THREE TALES

GUSTAVE FLAUBERT, the younger son of a provincial doctor, was born in the town of Rouen in 1821. While still a schoolboy, full of romantic scorn for the bourgeois world, he professed himself 'disgusted with life'. At the age of eighteen he was sent to study law in Paris, but had no regrets when a mysterious nervous ailment interrupted this career after only three years. Flaubert retired to live with his widowed mother in the family home at Croisset, on the banks of the river Seine, near Rouen. Supported by a private income, he devoted himself to his writing.

In his early work, particularly *The Temptation of Saint Antony*, he gave free rein to his flamboyant imagination, but on the advice of his friends he subsequently disciplined this romantic exuberance in an effort to achieve artistic objectivity and a harmonious prose style. This perfectionism cost him enormous toil and brought him only limited success in his own lifetime. After the publication of *Madame Bovary* in 1857 he was prosecuted for offending public morals; his exotic novel *Salammbô* (1862) was criticized for its encrustations of archaeological detail; *Sentimental Education* (1869), intended as the moral history of his generation, was largely misunderstood by the critics; and the political play *The Candidate* (1874) was a disastrous failure. Only *Three Tales* (1877) was an unqualified success, but it appeared when Flaubert's spirits, health and finances were all at their lowest ebb.

After his death in 1880 Flaubert's fame and reputation grew steadily, strengthened by the publication of his unfinished comic masterpiece *Bouvard and Pécuchet* (1881) and the many remarkable volumes of his correspondence.

ROGER WHITEHOUSE studied French at Oxford and at the University of Warwick, specializing in Renaissance studies. He taught at the Ecole Normale Supérieure and the Sorbonne, and from 1970 to 2000 at Bolton Institute. He was for many years Head of Literary Studies there and since 2000 has been a research fellow. He is currently working on a translation of Zola's *La Bête humaine* and is editing an anthology of the work of Emile Verhaeren.

GEOFFREY WALL is a literary biographer, travel writer and transla-
tor. His biography of Flaubert was published to great acclaim in
2001. His translations of Flaubert, published by Penguin Books,
include *Madame Bovary* (1992), *The Dictionary of Received Ideas*
(1994), *Selected Letters* (1996) and *Sentimental Education* (2004).
He is currently writing a biography of Napoleon.

GUSTAVE FLAUBERT
Three Tales

Translated by ROGER WHITEHOUSE
With an Introduction and Notes by
GEOFFREY WALL

PENGUIN BOOKS

PENGUIN BOOKS

Published by the Penguin Group
Penguin Books Ltd, 80 Strand, London WC2R ORL, England
Penguin Group (USA) Inc., 375 Hudson Street, New York, New York 10014, USA
Penguin Books Australia Ltd, 250 Camberwell Road, Camberwell, Victoria 3124, Australia
Penguin Books Canada Ltd, 10 Alcorn Avenue, Toronto, Ontario, Canada M4V 3B2
Penguin Books India (P) Ltd, 11 Community Centre, Panchsheel Park, New Delhi – 110 017, India
Penguin Group (NZ), cnr Airborne and Rosedale Roads, Albany, Auckland 1310, New Zealand
Penguin Books (South Africa) (Pty) Ltd, 24 Sturdee Avenue, Rosebank 2196, South Africa

Penguin Books Ltd, Registered Offices: 80 Strand, London WC2R ORL, England

www.penguin.com

First published as *Trois contes* 1877
First published in Penguin Classics 2005

021

Translation copyright © Roger Whitehouse, 2005
Editorial material copyright © Geoffrey Wall, 2005
All rights reserved

Set in 10.25/12.25 pt PostScript Adobe Sabon
Typeset by Rowland Phototypesetting Ltd, Bury St Edmunds, Suffolk
Printed and bound in Great Britain by Clays Ltd, Elcograf S.p.A.

ISBN-13: 978-0-140-44800-9

www.greenpenguin.co.uk

Penguin Books is committed to a sustainable
future for our business, our readers and our planet.
This book is made from Forest Stewardship
Council™ certified paper.

Contents

Chronology

1802 Achille Flaubert, Gustave's father, arrives in Paris to study medicine.

1810 Achille Flaubert moves to Rouen to work as deputy head of the hospital (known as the Hôtel-Dieu).

1812 Achille Flaubert marries the adopted daughter of the head of the Hôtel-Dieu.

1813 Birth of Achille-Cléophas, Gustave's brother.

1819 Achille Flaubert appointed head of Hôtel-Dieu on the death of his superior. The family moves to the residential wing of the hospital.

1820 Achille Flaubert begins to buy parcels of land and property outside Rouen.

1821 December: birth of Gustave Flaubert.

1824 July: birth of Caroline Flaubert, Gustave's sister.

1825 The servant 'Julie' enters the service of the Flaubert family.

1830 First surviving letter by Flaubert.

1832 Enters Collège de Rouen as a boarder. Creation of *Le Garçon*, an anarchic Rabelaisian joker.

1835 Summer holidays on the coast, at Trouville. Meets the Collier family.

1836 First encounter with Elisa Schlésinger, on the beach at Trouville.

1839 Elder brother qualifies in medicine and marries.

1840 Passes final school examinations; voyage to Corsica with Jules Cloquet. *Amour de voyage*, in Marseille, with Eulalie Foucaud.

1841 November: registers as law student in Paris, though continues to live at home.

1842 July: moves to Paris. December: passes first-year law exams.

1843 February: writing early version of *L'Education sentimentale (Sentimental Education)*. March: first meeting with Maxime Du Camp. August: fails second-year law exams.

1844 January: first nervous attack. April: father buys house at Croisset. June: Flaubert family moves to Croisset.

1845 March: sister marries Émile Hamard. April–June: family travelling in Italy. November: father falls ill.

1846 January: father dies; sister gives birth to a daughter. March: sister dies. July: first encounter with Louise Colet; marriage of Alfred Le Poittevin. August: begins friendship with Louis Bouilhet; first letter to Louise Colet.

1847 May–August: walking tour in Brittany with Maxime Du Camp.

1848 February: arrives in Paris, with Bouilhet, to see the street-fighting. April: death of Alfred Le Poittevin. May: begins work on first version of *La Tentation de Saint Antoine (The Temptation of Saint Antony)*. August: break with Louise Colet. September: finishes first version of *Saint Antoine*. October: embarks with Du Camp on eighteen-month tour of the Orient.

1850 February: voyage up the Nile. May: crossing the desert by camel. August: death of Balzac; Flaubert and Du Camp arrive in Jerusalem. September: plan for journey to Persia abandoned; the travellers turn west. October: Rhodes. November: Constantinople. December: Athens.

1851 April: Flaubert in Rome; Du Camp returns to Paris. May: Flaubert arrives home in Croisset; resumes relations with Louise Colet. September: begins writing *Madame Bovary*.

1852 January: Du Camp awarded Légion d'honneur. September: Du Camp becomes editor of the *Revue de Paris*.

1853 September: death of père Parain, a favourite uncle.

1854 October: final break with Louise Colet.

1855 October: takes rooms in Paris.

1856 April: finishes *Madame Bovary*. May: rewriting *Saint Antoine*. October: first instalment of *Madame Bovary* published in *Revue de Paris*.

1857 January: Flaubert prosecuted for publishing an immoral book. February: *Bovary* trial ends in acquittal. April: *Madame Bovary* published in book form. October: begins work on *Salammbô*.

1858 April–June: visits Carthage and North Africa, site of *Salammbô*.

1862 February: finishes *Salammbô*. November: *Salammbô* published.

1863 January: first letter to George Sand. February: first meeting with Turgenev.

1864 January: niece Caroline engaged to Ernest Commainville. May: begins work on new version of *L'Education sentimentale*. November: first visit to Compiègne as guest of the Emperor.

1866 August: nominated Chevalier de la Légion d'honneur. November: George Sand's first visit to Croisset.

1868 May: George Sand staying in Croisset.

1869 May: finishes *L'Education sentimentale*. July: death of Louis Bouilhet. November: publication of *L'Education sentimentale*. December: spends Christmas with George Sand in Nohant.

1870 August: beginning of Franco-Prussian war. December: victorious German troops arrive in Rouen.

1871 January: armistice signed with Prussia. May: insurrection in Paris. July: German troops leave Rouen.

1872 April: death of Flaubert's mother. June: finishes final version of *Saint Antoine*.

1874 March: *Saint Antoine* published. August: begins writing *Bouvard et Pécuchet*.

1875 Bad health and financial problems. September: begins writing 'La Légende de Saint Julien l'Hospitalier'.

1876 March: death of Louise Colet. June: death of George Sand. August: finishes writing 'Un Coeur simple'. November: begins work on 'Hérodias'.

1877 April: publication of *Trois contes* (*Three Tales*).

1879 October: awarded official pension.

1880 February: Du Camp elected to the Académie française. May: death of Flaubert.

1881 House at Croisset is sold and subsequently demolished to make way for a distillery.

1882 January: death of brother, Achille Flaubert. Du Camp publishes his *Souvenirs littéraires*.

1884 Publication of first volume of Flaubert's letters.

Introduction

What kind of writer is Flaubert? A satirist, like Voltaire and De
Sade? A realist, like Joyce and Kafka? Or a romantic, like Byron
and Victor Hugo? More to the point, why are there no real
artists, no official representatives of dishevelled genius in any of
his books?

Consider Flaubert at the age of 25, as revealed in his letters.
He is mildly grandiose, magnificently dishevelled and perfectly
confident. Though still unpublished, he knows the kind of writer
he wants to be and already he can project a splendidly intense
romantic persona. Here he is, in October 1846, writing to his
new lover, Louise Colet: 'I am the obscure, tenacious pearl-diver
who explores the lower depths and surfaces empty-handed, his
face turning blue. A fatal attraction pulls me towards the dark
places of the mind, down into the inner deep, so perpetually
enticing to the stout-hearted.'[1]

The lower depths? That was the place to begin.

Written three decades later, in the mid-1870s, Flaubert's
Three Tales display the final glistening catch. This is what the
pearl-diver has retrieved from those lower depths, after a lifetime
of staring heroically into the dark. Yet Flaubert's earliest French
readers may have felt slightly puzzled by this new offering. In
their daily paper, *Le Moniteur universel*, on the morning of
12 April 1877, they came upon the opening section of 'A Simple
Heart'. Like most serial fiction of the day, it was displayed in a
prominent position, spread across the lower portion of the front
page, in close competition with the news from the Balkans where
Russia was still uttering threats against Turkey.

Flaubert was a name long familiar to the discerning. Was this to be another spacious chronicle of modern life, like *Sentimental Education*? Or was it some exotic fantasy with a girl and big snake. Another *Salammbô*? It was neither. It appeared to be a story about a loyal family servant of rather limited imagination and intelligence. But surely Balzac had done all this long ago. Could it be that the champion of contemporary realism had grown weary of his larger ambitions? Was this some autumnal *jeu d'esprit* from the author of *Madame Bovary*? A lamentable subsiding into middle age?

On the contrary. Flaubert's *Three Tales* are his impulsive and triumphant finale. 'The best thing you've ever written', according to the author's sceptical, worldly wise older brother, Achille.

Yet it was a most improbable triumph, if we consider the dismal facts that stand just behind the writing of *Three Tales*. In his early fifties, Flaubert's tranquil, contemplative, daily life had been turned upside down. His troubles began in the autumn of 1870, when France suffered a ruinous military defeat at the hands of Prussia. In his large house by the river Seine, Flaubert soon found himself playing host to half a dozen victorious Prussian officers and their horses. The Prussian officers required the author of *Madame Bovary* to go out foraging for hay. They requisitioned his wine-cellar. They squandered his winter store of firewood. Worst of all, they left behind them a faint but troubling smell of riding-boots.

The next few years piled ever greater injuries upon his head. In 1872, bewildered by the war, Flaubert's fragile domineering mother died. She left the lovely big house (*his* lovely big house) to her penny-wise niece, Caroline, rather than her spendthrift son. Then in 1874 Flaubert's long-cherished closet-drama, *The Temptation of Saint Antony*, was published to a general chorus of mockery and misunderstanding. His other achievement, a topical political comedy, *The Candidate*, was simultaneously jeered off the Paris stage. Finally, in 1875, most of Flaubert's inherited capital vanished in noble but entirely futile efforts to save his niece's husband from bankruptcy. Meanwhile his current project, a novel about two copy clerks called *Bouvard and Pécuchet*, was going very badly.

What was he to do, now that the material conditions of his insidiously exquisite style had melted into the air? He needed something simple, to restore his morale and propel him forwards. Some thirty years before, he had worked on a little medieval tale about Saint Julian, a story sparked by the contemplation of a stained-glass window in a local church. That was the way to go. A collection of stories to connect with a new audience. He could sell them to the newspapers. He might make some money.

Prompted by adversity, the tales came quickly. Yet they are wonderfully impersonal in their chronicle of profit and loss. Their undeclared theme is abjection and all the ambiguous visions that crowd upon the mind as it falls into the dark. They each portray a certain religious experience, but they do this in the contemporary secular idiom of the novel. Like Frazer's *The Golden Bough*, Freud's *The Interpretation of Dreams* and Conrad's *Heart of Darkness*, all published around the end of the century, Flaubert's *Three Tales* show how the sacred survives, oddly disguised, even in the century of wide-awake bourgeois techno-miracles.

Discreetly but cheerfully defying the sober imperatives of the age, Flaubert was the provincial bourgeois who lived a hundred lives. *Cet original de Monsieur Flaubert* – 'that peculiar Monsieur Flaubert'. That was how citizens of Rouen referred to him, if they could bring themselves to speak his name. More charitable than his contemporaries, we might see him sitting at his large circular writing-table, with his dish of quills, hammering and polishing his sentences into shape, hour after hour. Or he is sprawled on his green morocco leather couch, like some voluptuously indolent deity riding on a great cloud, picturing his creatures, fashioning a world for them. Yet he is never perfectly at home in any of these worlds. He is always divided between the imagined and the real, flitting between the ramparts of ancient Carthage and the boulevards of industrial Rouen.

Such reckless mobility. It was a curse. A visionary talent. Or perhaps it was just a joke.

When Flaubert described his agreeably nomadic condition to George Sand, it looked a mixture of all three. 'I feel as if I've existed for ever,' he told her in 1866.

> I possess memories that go back to the Pharaohs. I can see myself very clearly at different moments in history, following different trades, according to my luck. My present self is the outcome of all my extinct selves. I was a boatman on the Nile, a pimp in Rome at the time of the Punic wars, then a Greek orator in Suburra where I was devoured by bed-bugs. I died during the Crusades from eating too many grapes on a beach in Syria. I have been a pirate and a monk, an acrobat and a coachman. Emperor of the Orient too perhaps?[2]

These three tales allowed Flaubert to arrange an assortment of these 'extinct selves' within a clear frame. He could be a servant girl, a pious old woman, a warrior prince, a hermit in a hovel, a tyrant in a palace, a prophet in a dungeon. The pattern of these chosen reincarnations is interesting. They start very low and they end very high. The protagonists all go mad, and each tale ends with strange images of death. It's almost preposterous to encompass so much within three tales. Three is of course the superlative fairy-tale number. Three is just-enough-and-no-more, the number of repetition with variation. This three-ness lends the collection its compact and evocative shape. The audacious simplicity of their running title – *Three Tales* ... nothing more! – suggests completeness. In each tale the surface details are reassuringly plausible. By these strong, invisible threads, each tale draws us towards the dark and fearful places of the mind.

Flaubert had already travelled this way twice before. First with his Carthaginian novel, *Salammbô*, and then with his closet-drama, *The Temptation of Saint Antony*. These efforts had foundered in a lavish but stagnant exoticism, like so many earnest nineteenth-century visions of the pre-bourgeois. Yet Flaubert was sure that a great fictional subject was to be

found somewhere hereabouts. 'I am convinced', he wrote in
1859,

> that the most furious material appetites are expressed *unknow-ingly* by flights of idealism, just as the most sordidly extravagant
> sexual acts are engendered by a pure desire for the impossible, an
> ethereal aspiration after sovereign joy. I do not know (nobody
> knows) the meaning of the words body and soul, where the one
> ends and the other begins. We feel *the play of energy* and that is
> all ... The anatomy of the human heart has not yet been done
> ... recently I have come back to those psycho-medical studies
> which I found so fascinating ten years ago ... There are treasures
> yet to be found in all of that.[3]

Within forty years, the new science of psychoanalysis would
confirm Flaubert's sketchmap of the unconscious.

The younger son of a renowned man of science, Flaubert had
long cultivated a mildly perverse taste for the supernatural. He
acquired it in his earliest years, before he could read, from his
peasant-nursemaid, Julie. Though regarded as a simple daughter
of the people, Julie was exceptionally intelligent and well read.
Fortunately for the child in her care, she was also more spon-
taneously affectionate than his natural mother, the melancholy
Madame Flaubert. Julie sat the boy by the kitchen fire and told
him wonderful stories, stories that took him far away from
Rouen, back into an older rural world. Here was a night-world
where the giant Gargantua walked the earth, where druid stones
came alive and great snakes lay coiled asleep in dark pools. Julie
knew all about talking animals, elves and changeling children,
goblins, werewolves, witches and – most memorable of all –
decapitated saints, the kind that were found wandering along
lonely country roads carrying their own heads in little baskets.
    Here was something wonderful, something more nourish-
ing than the desiccated rationalism that shaped all significant
conversation within the municipal hospital, the Hôtel-Dieu,
that temple of science where his father, the compassionate,
omnipotent, Monsieur Flaubert, presided so illustriously.

Though he avoided writing about childhood, Flaubert never abandoned the high kingdom of miracles and prodigies that had so precociously excited his imagination. 'Early impressions', he wrote, 'never fade . . . We carry our past within us; all our lives we still smell of our nurse's milk.'[4] The memory of Julie, the generous smiling story-teller who warmed the cold hours of his boyhood, lay preserved in his mind. Loyal to these early visions, Flaubert accumulated a vast leisurely adult erudition on the subject of saints, heretics and goddesses. The supernatural was his second home, though he arrived there through a door marked *science*.

Imagination, for all its idle splendours, doesn't pay the bills. The great city of Rouen was energetic testimony to this simple fact. As the younger son of a great man, Gustave Flaubert was expected to add lustre to the family name. The medical profession had already been allocated to Achille, the eldest son. Gustave would therefore be directed into the study of the law. At this point, on the threshold of everything sensible, bourgeois and masculine, his problems began.

'Studying Law', Flaubert soon complained, 'leaves me in a state of moral castration which is almost inconceivable.'[5] The phrase was not lightly chosen. As a young man, away from home for the first time, Flaubert was 'imperiously possessed' by the idea of castrating himself. 'In the midst of all my vexation in Paris . . . I wanted to do it.' He would stare at mutilated male statues in museums, struggling with the impulse to mutilate himself.[6] He resisted the 'mystic mania', as he called it, and chose instead to avoid 'seeing women', a resolution that lasted for several years.[7]

What was it, the problem to which castration seemed to be the imperative solution? We do not know, and nor did Flaubert. We do know that a traumatic experience of sacred horror is at the heart of his 'exotic' works. We may wonder at the mature artist's abiding impulse to play with fire. Flaubert's finest characters are visionaries, passionately materialized. They are not quite of this world, though the mud of the real will cling thick and heavy to their boots. Like their creator, they are pestered, tormented, amazed and bewildered by their visions. Unlike their creator, they are finally consumed by the power of what they see.

Flaubert improvised many ingenious solutions to this problem. In the middle of writing *Madame Bovary*, kicking against the constraints of the genre, he had envisaged 'a large fantastical loudmouth metaphysical novel'[8] which would prove that 'happiness is in the imagination'. In real life the hero would be reviled, imprisoned, and ultimately thrown into a lunatic asylum; but in his imagined life he would achieve a triumphant serenity. The story would be called 'La Spirale'. It evolved over many years, in the background, as 'a novel about madness, or rather about *the way* in which you go mad'.[9] Yet 'La Spirale' remained unwritten: 'because it is a subject that frightens me, for health reasons, I shall have to wait until I am far enough away from those experiences to be able to induce them in myself artificially, ideally, and therefore without risk to myself or to my work.'[10] A loudmouth metaphysical novel about madness would be too close to home.

Fear of madness had preyed upon Flaubert's mind ever since a singular episode that took place one evening in his student days. The story of that evening explains much of Flaubert's persistent interest in other worlds of experience, and it is offered here, as a biographical preface to his *Three Tales*.

One January evening (let the year be 1844) two young men were driving along a French country road in a lightweight two-wheeled cabriolet. Gustave Flaubert, the younger and the sturdier of the pair, was holding the reins. Sitting beside him was his slender, red-bearded elder brother, Achille, a man whom Flaubert rather disliked. The moonless winter night was unusually dark and the puddles in the ditches were growing a fragile skin of ice. 'It was so dark,' he said, 'you couldn't even see the horse's ears' – a real, cave-black, supernatural, nineteenth-century pre-electric dark, with only the light of a distant inn to dispel the perfect illusion of nothingness.

The little cabriolet turned a corner and the brothers heard a rumbling and a jingling coming towards them. It was the

iron-bound wheels of a big wagon carrying a single night-lantern
up in front. The bright flame of the lantern on the wagon moved
slowly across their field of vision, away from the distant light of
the inn. The conjunction of the two lights, near and far, moving
and stationary, sparked something inside the skull of the big
man holding the reins of the cabriolet. It was, he said, like an
explosion behind his eyes, 'like being swept away in a torrent of
flames ... sudden as lightning ... an instantaneous irruption
of *memory* ... a letting go of its entire contents. You feel the
images pouring out of you like a stream of blood ... as if
everything in your head is going off at once like a thousand
fireworks.'[11] Gustave Flaubert fell to the floor of the cabriolet
and lay there as if he were dead. He was 22 years old.

His family hoped that it was all an accident, unlikely to
happen again. But it was no accident. It came back. In the course
of the next two weeks Flaubert had four further attacks. What
had happened to him? What name could medical science give
to the golden fire that had burnt such a dark hole in the fabric
of his life? Was it epilepsy? Apoplexy? Hysteria? Or was it
simply 'nerves'?

For Flaubert himself, there was no word for it. 'Never', said
his friend Maxime Du Camp, 'did I hear him speak the name
of his malady. He said, "my nervous attacks", and that was
all.'[12] Such reluctance is not surprising. Epilepsy was not understood. The symptoms of the disease had been described in
antiquity, by Hippocrates, but there was still no effective treatment for it. It was a hopeless, loathsome, incomprehensible
thing and its victims were subjected to a drastic regime. In
Flaubert's case, a device like a small tap, known as a seton
collar, was attached to his neck to facilitate regular bleeding.
Purgative mercury massages were applied. Alcohol, tobacco,
caffeine and meat were forbidden. The patient was secluded and
carefully watched over.

The treatment wore a rational modern disguise. Yet from
beneath that disguise it spoke in the older language of religious
symbolism. However unscientific to our eyes, it makes good
sense if we consider it as a ritual of purification. Victim and
family moved out to Croisset, a holy place beside a great river,

thus escaping all the malignant impurities that hung in the air of the city. At Croisset the victim was symbolically cleansed of his pollution, through repeated washing, bloodletting and swimming.

Flaubert subsequently observed and described his nameless condition with great acuity. We might say, from the evidence of his letters, that he learnt to live with it, to inhabit it imaginatively as a unique province of his mind. Perhaps a name would have kept him out, discouraged him from undertaking that terrifying quest. Once he knew that he could survive the recurrent intimate disaster of the attack, he could begin to learn from it, even to experiment with it. His epilepsy, or rather what he did with what they called epilepsy, confirmed in him a curious early affinity for the most extreme varieties of religious experience, the ecstatic visions and the diabolical torments of the saints.

It was George Sand, Flaubert's generously sympathetic confidante, who urged Flaubert to make something of his sufferings. 'Describe your martyrdom,' she wrote in January 1875. 'There is a fine book to be written there.'[13] Reluctantly won over to the idea, Flaubert did not begin with a flamboyantly dramatic martyrdom – the obvious, fiery-torment, agony-in-the-desert variety. He had done that already, in *The Temptation of Saint Antony*. There was another kind of martyrdom, the slow stifling of the spirit, the quiet sinking into decrepitude. This was the modern martyrdom. He had, after all, recently witnessed the mental and physical dissolution of his mother during the final years of her life. He could feel in his own mind the first keen vexations of old age: his friends dying, his money disappearing, his house falling apart, his faculties decaying. Here was a subject close to home.

He had a clear sense of what he wanted his martyr-tale to be. Its 'underlying humanity'[14] would confound all those who had ever chided him for treating his characters sadistically. This time there would be no amputations, no arsenic poisoning, no flaying of captives, no dead babies (not in the first story, at least; there would be plenty of that sort of thing in the other two tales). This would be the intimate history of the love that never found an object. He would draw upon the scenes of his own early years: the seaside holiday landscapes, the memories of his younger sister who had died. He would borrow the forlorn, frozen egocentricities of his mother's lengthy widowhood. He would take the woman's part, as he had done once before, with Emma Bovary.

Feminization was much better than castration. It was reversible and it connected him to all that was most radically original in his own artistic personality. He would become a servant, pious, illiterate and loving. 'The Story of a Simple Heart', he explained,

> is quite simply the tale of the obscure life of a poor country girl, devout but not given to mysticism, devoted in a quiet sober way and soft as newly baked bread. One after the other she loves a man, her mistress's children, a nephew, an old man she nurses, then her parrot; when the parrot dies she has it stuffed, and when she is on her deathbed she takes the parrot for the Holy Ghost. It is in no way ironic (though you might suppose it to be so) but on the contrary very serious and very sad. I want to move my readers to pity, I want to make sensitive souls weep, being one myself.[15]

Flaubert's denial of ironic intention is persuasive, but also amusingly devious. He wants to protect this icon of mother-love from attack, even though he knows it's a bit ridiculous. This makes for delicate tension in the texture of his story. The writing invites us to renounce the agreeable intellectual aggression that we call irony. Are we too clever, it asks us, to sit down quietly among the simple-hearted? Is their silence too much for us? Is our cherished irony just a bad habit? Is the head censoring the heart? Flaubert always leaves such questions unspoken, but they mark out a serious imaginative problem for realist art and for democratic politics. How can we represent the dispossessed, the illiterate and the powerless? Yes, we give them a voice. But whose voice is it to be? Their voice, or our version of their voice?

Flaubert had glanced at this problem once before. In the middle of *Madame Bovary*, there is a village agricultural show. The local elite are sitting up on the platform, announcing prizes.

They summon before them 'a little old woman'. For a lifetime of agricultural labour, she is to receive a silver medal. She is a vision of compliant servitude.

Then was seen stepping on to the platform a little old woman, moving timidly, and apparently cringing deep into her shabby clothes. On her feet she had great wooden clogs, and, around her hips, a large blue apron. Her thin face, swathed in a simple hood, was more creased and wrinkled than a withered russet apple, and from the sleeves of her red camisole there dangled a pair of long hands, with bony knuckles. The dust from the barn, the soda for washing and the grease from wool had made them crusted, cracked, calloused, so that they looked grimy even though they had been rinsed in fresh water; and, from long service, they stayed half unclasped, almost as though to set forth of themselves the simple testimony of so much affliction endured. A hint of monastic rigidity intensified the look on her face. No touch of sadness or affection softened that pale gaze. Living close to the animals, she had assumed their wordless placid state of being. It was the first time she had found herself in the midst of such a large gathering; and, inwardly terrified by the flags, by the drums, by the gentlemen in frock coats, and by the councillor's Legion of Honour medal, she stood quite still not knowing whether to step forwards or to run away, nor why the crowd were pushing her on and the judges smiling at her. There she stood, before these flourishing bourgeois, this half-century of servitude.[16]

In this strange antithetical figure Flaubert sketches out something quite remarkable, though at this point he is not yet sure what he wants to do with it artistically. As the contemporary (though scarcely the admirer) of the realist painter Gustave Courbet, Flaubert wanted to push at the legal limits of realism. Others may write compassionately of the poor. Such anguished compassion is a nineteenth-century speciality. But how is this to be done without idealizing the wretched? Without turning them into angels of virtue, or monsters of vice?

Flaubert has a special interest which serves him well. Always ready to adopt weaker vessels as his protagonists – there is

nothing exemplary, nothing special, about his Emma or his Fréd-
éric in *Sentimental Education* – he is satirically but authentically
fascinated by idiots, by their 'wordless placid state of being',
'close to the animals'. The saintly stupidity of Félicité, servant-
heroine of 'A Simple Heart', will draw out the superior clever-
ness of those all around her. Surviving every loss, every insult,
without serious complaint, without fine phrases, she can display
a primitive moral grandeur which is teasingly instructive.

Flaubert had installed a stuffed parrot on his writing desk, to
assist him in the composition of 'A Simple Heart'. 'At the
moment,' he told his niece, 'I'm writing with an "Amazon"
standing on my writing table, his beak askew, gazing at me
with his glass eyes. [...] The sight of the thing is beginning to annoy me. But I'm keeping him there, to fill my mind
with the idea of parrothood.'[17] The parrot in Flaubert's story
would be called *Loulou*, a name which undoubtedly had a
certain resonance for the author. *Loulou* was the pet-name
for his niece, Caroline. And Caroline was a name that went
back three generations. *Loulou* meant love and affection, happy
domesticity, the unbroken maternal line.

Flaubert's parrot has overshadowed the other figure who
contributed significantly to 'A Simple Heart'. Frail and ancient,
the family servant Julie was still in service in the spring of 1876
when Flaubert began writing his tale. After the death of his
mother, the solitary grieving son had given Julie a selection of
the dresses that had once belonged to her, thus creating for
himself a ghostly composite figure of the maternal virtues. It is
interesting, though it may be mere coincidence, that Julie arrived
in Croisset in the same week as the more famous parrot. We
catch sight of Julie in Flaubert's letters. Thin and frail, delighted
to be in Croisset 'for the country air', she is now completely
blind and a child is employed to lead her around the garden.[18]

Invigorated by the extraordinary August heat, Flaubert
worked on 'A Simple Heart' with a singular passion. On his
table, alongside the stuffed parrot, he had laid out the raw
materials for his story's ending: a medical treatise on pneumonia, a breviary and a collection of prayer-books.[19] He had

entered a realm of mysterious intellectual exaltation. He was working his phrases while swimming in the Seine and then in his sleep the words were still coming to him: 'In the night the sentences go rolling through my mind, like the chariots of some Roman emperor, and they wake me with a start by their jolting and their endless rumbling.'[20] He was often writing all through the night, with the windows open, in his shirt sleeves, 'bellowing like a fiend, in the silence of my study', bellowing until his lungs were hurting and he saw the dawn. 'One day,' he joked, 'I shall explode like an artillery shell and all my bits will be found on the writing table.'[21]

'A Simple Heart' celebrates the maternal virtues. In Madame Aubain's damp and half-empty house, paternal authority has withered away and now Monsieur is no more than a memory, an old portrait on display in a room upstairs. The two subsequent tales investigate what happens when we call Father back from oblivion. Resurrected in the outsized garments of fantasy, Father now assumes two contrasting forms, one weak and one strong. In 'The Legend of Saint Julian Hospitator' he is a medieval lord, whose son will accidentally kill him. In 'Herodias' he is an Oriental patriarch, who will be tricked into killing the man who mocks his authority. In both tales, clearly visible just below the flamboyantly archaic surface, there is a twisted sexual motive driving the plot. For this is a world of lethal erotic caprice, massacre, mutilation, accidental parricide and decapitation. Obviously Oedipal, we say, staring our author in the eye. Yet this is an Oedipus with a difference. For Flaubert treats his crew of saints, prophets and patriarchs with a thoroughly modern ambivalence, subjecting their visions to the mildly corrosive secular action of the realist style.

'The Legend of Saint Julian Hospitator' culminates in a miraculous, intimate, deathly reconciliation with the father. Assuming the form of a decomposing leper, the father arrives from nowhere and demands from his son the signs of love: food and drink, a warm bed, a comforting embrace, a contaminating kiss. It is too much, an impossible moment. Touching the father inspires a powerful sexual disgust in his son, tinged with terror and yet rewarded with a surprise-ticket to heaven. At this point Flaubert famously breaks the frame of his story, abruptly disavowing the scene he has imagined: 'And that is the story of Saint Julian Hospitator almost exactly as you will find it told in a stained-glass window in a church near to where I was born.'

Nowhere else, in all his fiction, does Flaubert ever show his hand in this way. He is professionally invisible. What are we to make of this bizarre exception?

There is indeed a Saint Julian window in the cathedral at Rouen, and the cathedral is indeed only half a mile from the house where Flaubert was born. That much is true. But if we compare the pictures in the window with the principal features of the tale we are baffled by the disparity between image and text. Flaubert pictured the probable scene with some relish. In a letter to his publisher, discussing the possibility of an illustrated edition of 'The Legend of Saint Julian Hospitator', Flaubert imagined his readers saying: 'I don't understand it at all. How did he get *this* out of *that*?' The last sentence of the tale is evidently a kind of joke, a piece of solemn authorial mischief that works at many different levels.

Rather than puzzling over the window we might do better to look at the thirteenth-century text of the legend of Saint Julian. Here it is, as translated and published by William Caxton, in 1483.

Another Julian there was that slew his father and mother by ignorance. And this man was noble and young, and gladly went for to hunt. And one time among all other he found an hart which returned toward him, and said to him, thou huntest me that shall slay thy father and mother. Hereof was he much abashed and afeard, and for dread, that it should not happen to him that the hart had said to him, he went privily away that no man knew thereof, and found a prince noble and great to whom he put him in service. And he proved so well in battle and in services in his palace, that he was so much in the prince's grace that he made him knight and gave to him a rich widow of a castle, and for her dower he received the castle. And when his father and mother knew that he was thus gone they put them in the way for to seek

him in many places. And so long they went till they came to the
castle where he dwelt, but then he was gone out, and they found
his wife. And when she saw them she inquired diligently who they
were, and when they had said and recounted what was happened
of their son, she knew verily that they were the father and mother
of her husband, and received them much charitably, and gave to
them her own bed, and made another for herself. And on the
morn the wife of Julian went to the church, and her husband
came home whiles she was at church, and entered into his chamber
for to awake his wife. And he saw twain in his bed, and had
weened that it had been a man that had lain with his wife, and
slew them both with his sword, and after, went out and saw
his wife coming from church. Then he was much abashed and
demanded of his wife who they were that lay in his bed, then she
said that they were his father and his mother, which had long
sought him, and she had laid them in his bed. Then he swooned
and was almost dead, and began to weep bitterly and cry, alas!
caitiff that I am, what shall I do that have slain my father and my
mother? Now it is happened that I supposed to have eschewed,
and said to his wife: Adieu and farewell, my right dear love, I
shall never rest till that I shall have knowledge if God will pardon
and forgive me this that I have done, and that I shall have worthy
penance therefor. And she answered: Right dear love, God forbid
that ye should go without me, like as I have had joy with you, so
will I have pain and heaviness. Then departed they and went till
they came to a great river over which much folk passed, where
they edified an hospital much great for to harbour poor people,
and there do their penance in bearing men over that would pass.

After long time S. Julian slept about midnight, sore travailed,
and it was frozen and much cold, and he heard a voice lamenting
and crying that said: Julian come and help us over. And anon he
arose, and went over and found one almost dead for cold, and
anon he took him and bare him to the fire and did great labour
to chauffe and warm him. And when he saw that he could not be
chauffed ne warm, he bare him in to his bed, and covered him the
best wise he might. And anon after, he that was so sick and
appeared as he had been measell, he saw all shining ascending to
heaven, and said to S. Julian his host: Julian, our Lord hath sent

me to thee, and sendeth thee word that he hath accepted thy penance. And a while after S. Julian and his wife rendered unto God their souls and departed out of this world.

Flaubert's 'Legend of Saint Julian Hospitator' evidently follows the outline of the original legend. But there is one very big difference. This Julian is obsessed with hunting. As a young boy he discovers a perfectly lascivious pleasure in the killing of small animals. He then carves his way through the entire catalogue of the animal kingdom, a veritable massacre of the innocents, beginning with a little white mouse and ending with a large and majestic stag. Flaubert's version of the hunting theme is explicitly sadistic. We are made to watch as Julian strangles a wounded pigeon, fainting with pleasure as he feels the creature's final convulsions. Yet Flaubert is infinitely more imaginative than any of De Sade's cartoon-like tormentors. In this tale he has the creatures turn against their persecutor, driving him into a state of impotent rage. In this condition he murders his father and mother, by mistake.

Where does it come from, the extraneous theme of Julian's sadism? Is it the sour exhalation of his creator? There is plausible evidence for this possibility. And yet Flaubert's sadism, if we must call it that, is uncomfortably complex, for it struggles with a benevolent compassion.

A dream dating from 1845, when Flaubert was in his early twenties, dramatizes this original ambivalence. The dream was written down, so Flaubert explained, three weeks after it had been dreamt. The delay hints at the persistent power of the dream. It also implies that the original material of the dream had been variously worked over, in the waking imagination, before Flaubert told himself to put it all in writing. Here is the text of the dream.

I was in a great forest full of monkeys; my mother was walking with me. The further we went the more there were; they were up in the branches, laughing and jumping about; they came across our path, lots of them, bigger and bigger, more and more of them. They were all looking at me and I began to feel frightened. They gathered around us in a circle; one of them wanted to stroke me and took my hand, I gave it a bullet in the shoulder that made it bleed and it made a dreadful howling noise. Then my mother said to me, 'Why did you hurt him when he's your friend? What's he done to you? Can't you see that he loves you? He looks so like you!' And the monkey was looking at me. It broke my heart and I woke up ... feeling my own deep affinity with the animals, fraternising with them in a tender pantheistic union.[22]

The essential ingredients of the dream – the fear, the killing, the reproach, the sorrow, the reparation – have been preserved, elaborated and disguised in the story. Thirty years after the initiating dream, Flaubert was unusually careful to give nothing away about this his most darkly enigmatic work. In the letters that he wrote alongside 'The Legend of Saint Julian Hospitator' he ridiculed the whole enterprise. It was merely 'a little religioso-poetico-medievalesque-rococo storyette', so delightfully edifying that its author will be suspected of lapsing into clericalism.[23]

The mockery is a way of saying *Keep Out*. Saint Julian was a subject he had chosen long ago. By the time Flaubert came to write about it, it had been with him for most of his life. Slowly and fondly elaborated, Flaubert's saint was a half-private creation, a secret thing of his own that might one day be passed off as a Saint Julian. Had he chosen it? Or had it chosen him? He sometimes confessed, jokingly, that it was probably the latter.

'Herodias', the final tale in the collection, is an exotic fable of sexual-political corruption, the grand finale of Flaubert's romantic orientalism, that unstable nineteenth-century compound of erotic reverie and conscientious erudition. The art market of Flaubert's day was already crowded with such exotica. The pre-bourgeois world furnished an ample supply of seductively colourful stuff, all available to be lucratively processed into grand opera, history painting, salon sculpture and fancy-dress fiction. By comparison with many of his contemporaries, Flaubert practises an exemplary sobriety. He works his large antique subject against the grain, avoiding the obvious, jumbling his rich narrative ingredients of religion and politics.

Readers of 'Herodias', however expert, will sometimes con-
fess to a certain confusion. But these confusions are deliberate,
a distinctive feature of the story. 'Herodias' is such an uncom-
monly elliptical piece of story-telling that it requires at least a
brief account of the larger political context to make it accessible
to the modern reader. 'Herodias' is set in Judaea (southern
Palestine), at the time of Christ's ministry. This is a world of
priests and kings. Great temples and fortresses dominate the
human scene. Subject to Rome, the Jewish people are smouldering with messianic hopes of liberation. Herod Antipas, their
puppet-king, and the protagonist of 'Herodias', is scheming to
ensure his own political survival. The king must urgently decide
what to do with his prisoner, a man referred to in the tale as
Jokanaan, though better known to posterity as John the Baptist.
(Flaubert's trick, here and elsewhere, is to divulge the familiar
name just once and then to suppress it, to make it strange again,
to tell the story in tight close-up, from within the narrow,
anxious mind of the king, a mind clouded by intrigue and
perfectly ignorant of the coming of Jesus.)

Herod Antipas (21 BC–AD 39) became Tetrarch (ruler
appointed by Rome) of Galilee and ruled throughout Jesus'
ministry. Herod Antipas is often referred to in the story as the
Tetrarch, or as Antipas. He divorced his first wife, daughter of
the king of the desert kingdom adjoining his own, to marry
his niece Herodias, formerly the wife of his half-brother. The
marriage offended his former father-in-law and alienated his
Jewish subjects. John the Baptist reproached Herod for this
marriage, as a transgression of Mosaic law. Herodias has goaded
her husband into imprisoning him. This is the point at which
Flaubert's tale begins.

'Herodias' reverses the larger pattern of 'The Legend of Saint
Julian Hospitator'. In this tale there is no parricide and no
reconciliation. The Father-King has had the Son-Prophet
imprisoned for denouncing his sexual-political corruption. Yet
the prophet's voice rises up from the deep hole in the ground,
condemning the king in the name of the moral law. The prophet
is murdered, at the king's command. This time there is no twist,
no supernatural escape from the prosaic reality of death and

mutilation. With the cruel humour of the folk tale, the decapitation of Jokanaan is a trick played on the king, a gruesome detumescent joke at his expense, brought about because he has lusted helplessly after a girl young enough to be his daughter. We are left gazing at this severed head, a 'gruesome object on the plate among the remains of the banquet'. The faithful will assert that the spirit of the prophet has 'gone down among the dead to proclaim the coming of Christ', but this severed head still poses a stubbornly practical problem for his disciples. They set off with it, in the direction of Galilee. 'Because the head was very heavy,' so says the last line of the story, 'they took it in turns to carry it.' A conclusion quite inscrutably prosaic.

Three Tales was surprisingly well reviewed in 1877. Here was recognition at last, though it came several years too late to assuage Flaubert's bitter sense of having been disregarded for so long. Here was a conspiracy of approval, gratifying of course, but also slightly embarrassing to an author who had been so resolutely misunderstood for the last ten years.

His reviewers praised the eloquent diversity of the collection. 'A Simple Heart' was wholesome and profoundly moving, something for the common reader. 'The Legend of Saint Julian Hospitator' offered the darker pleasures of the *conte fantastique*, so central to French romantic writing. 'Herodias' was the grand finale, a ripe autumnal specimen of the *conte orientale*, something for the connoisseur, cruel and magnificent, like a painting by Delacroix.

After *Madame Bovary*, this remains Flaubert's most immediately rewarding work. On the evidence of his *Three Tales*, Flaubert could plausibly claim to have reinvented the short story as well as the novel. His influence has been so pervasive that lists of his followers soon begin to look dubiously inflated. Here is my own dubious scratch crew of *Flaubertistes*: Guy de Maupassant, Emile Zola, Henry James, Kate Chopin, Anton Chekhov, Joseph Conrad, George Moore, Paul Valéry, James Joyce, Ezra Pound, Isaac Babel, Franz Kafka, Graham Greene, Albert Camus, Czeslaw Miłosz, Robert Lowell, Jean Rhys, Bruce Chatwin, Angela Carter and Raymond Carver. The list is not yet closed, because Flaubert remains our contemporary. Contemporary realism is still stubbornly Flaubertian, because we still need the peculiar intimate power of art, the power that sends strange shivers all through the majestically corpulent mass of the body politic.

NOTES

1. G. Flaubert, *Correspondance*, vol. 1, ed. J. Bruneau (Paris: Gallimard, 1973), p. 378.
2. Ibid., vol. 3 (1991), p. 536.
3. Ibid., pp. 16–17.
4. Ibid., vol. 1 (1973), p. 712.
5. Ibid., p. 120.
6. Ibid., vol. 2. (1980), p. 218.
7. J. Bruneau, *Les Débuts littéraires de Gustave Flaubert* (Paris: Armand Colin, 1962), p. 381, n. 96.
8. Flaubert, *Correspondance*, vol. 2 (1980), p. 285.
9. Ibid., vol. 3 (1991), p. 59.
10. Ibid., vol. 2 (1980), p. 290.
11. Ibid., vol. 3 (1991), p. 572.
12. M. Du Camp, *Souvenirs littéraires* (Paris: Hachette, 1882), vol. 1, p. 248.
13. Flaubert, *Correspondance*, vol. 4 (1998), p. 904.
14. *Flaubert–Sand: The Correspondence*, ed. A. Jacobs, trans. Francis Steegmuller and Barbara Bray (London: Harvill, 1993), p. 398.
15. G. Flaubert, *Œuvres complètes* (Paris: Club de l'Honnête homme, 1971–5), vol. 15, p. 458.
16. *Madame Bovary*, trans. G. Wall (Harmondsworth: Penguin, 1992), pp. 120–21.
17. Flaubert, *Œuvres complètes*, vol. 15, pp. 471, 476.
18. Ibid., p. 475.
19. Ibid., p. 480.
20. Ibid., p. 463.
21. Ibid., p. 481.
22. Quoted in A. W. Raitt, *Flaubert: Trois contes* (London: Grant and Cutler, 1991), pp. 54–5.
23. Flaubert, *Œuvres complètes*, vol. 15, p. 506.

Further Reading

Barnes, J., *Flaubert's Parrot* (London: Cape, 1984).

Berg, W. J., *Saint/Oedipus: Psychocritical Approaches to Flaubert's Art* (Ithaca, NY: Cornell University Press, 1982).

Brombert, V., *The Novels of Flaubert: A Study of Themes and Techniques* (Princeton: Princeton University Press, 1966).

Felman, S., 'Flaubert's Signature The Legend of Saint Julian the Hospitable', in Naomi Schor and Henry Majewski (eds.), *Flaubert and Postmodernism* (Lincoln: University of Nebraska Press, 1984), pp. 46–75.

Genette, G., 'Demotivation in Herodias', in Schor and Majewski (eds.), *Flaubert and Postmodernism*, pp. 193–201.

Raitt, A. W., 'The Composition of Flaubert's Saint Julien l'Hospitalier', *French Studies*, 19 (1965), pp. 358–72.

—— *Flaubert: Trois contes* (London: Grant and Cutler, 1991).

Wall, G., *Flaubert: A Life* (London: Faber, 2001).

Translator's Note

The translation is based on the 1988 Classiques Garnier edition of *Trois Contes* by P. M. Wetherill, which reproduces, in Professor Wetherill's words, 'as faithfully as possible, the text of Flaubert's final manuscript'.

Flaubert's final manuscript presents a considerable challenge to the editor. It is strewn with crossings-out, marginal notes and rewritings – a clear indication of Flaubert's search for historical, geographical and technical precision and for stylistic poise. Yet in his determination to get things just right, Flaubert left many finer points of expression (punctuation in particular) ill-defined. Since the first published edition of the collected tales in 1877, editors have attempted in different ways to make good these lapses. Professor Wetherill has produced an edition which is as close as can be to the author's own hand.

This translation is motivated by a similar concern. It seeks to maintain the precisely focused details of description and imagery, the tight ordering of sentences and the use of short detached paragraphs as Flaubert wrote them. Where a sentence has been re-ordered or where two sentences have been run together, this has been done to achieve a more natural rhythm or resonance in English, to discover as it were a speaking voice behind the written word. Flaubert himself tested the balance and fluency of his prose by reading it out aloud.

Three Tales

A SIMPLE HEART

For half a century, Madame Aubain's housemaid Félicité was the envy of all the good ladies of Pont-l'Evêque.

For just one hundred francs a year,[1] she did all the cooking and the housework, she saw to the darning, the washing and the ironing, she could bridle a horse, keep the chickens well fed and churn the butter. What is more she remained faithful to her mistress, who, it must be said, was not the easiest of people to get on with.

Madame Aubain had married a handsome but impecunious young man, who had died at the beginning of 1809, leaving her with two very young children and substantial debts. Upon his death, she sold her properties, with the exception of the two farms at Toucques and Geffosses,[2] which between them provided her with an income of no more than five thousand francs in rent, and she moved out of her house in Saint-Melaine to live in another which was less costly to maintain, which had belonged to her family and which was situated behind the market.

This house had a slate roof and stood between an alley and a narrow street leading down to the river. Inside, the floors were at different levels, making it very easy to trip up. A narrow hallway separated the kitchen from the living room in which Madame Aubain remained all day long, sitting in a wicker armchair close to the casement window. Against the wainscoting, which was painted white, there stood a row of eight mahogany chairs. A barometer hung on the wall above an old piano, piled high with a pyramid-shaped assortment of packets and cardboard boxes. Two easy chairs upholstered in tapestry stood on either side of a Louis-Quinze-style mantelpiece in yellow marble. The clock, in the middle, was designed to look like a Temple of Vesta,[3] and the whole room smelt musty, due to the fact that the floor level was lower than the garden.

On the first floor, there was 'Madame's' bedroom, a very large room, decorated with pale, flowery wallpaper and containing a picture of 'Monsieur' dressed up in the fanciful attire that was fashionable at the time. This room led directly to a smaller bedroom which housed two children's beds, each with the mattress removed. Next came the parlour, which was always kept locked and was full of furniture draped in dust-sheets. Finally, there was a corridor leading to a study; books and papers lay stacked on the shelves of a bookcase which ran around three walls of the room and surrounded a large writing-desk in dark wood. The two end panels of this bookcase were covered in line drawings, landscapes in gouache and etchings by Audran,[4] a reminder of better days and of more expensive tastes that were now a thing of the past. On the second floor was Félicité's bedroom, lit by a dormer window which looked out over the fields.

Félicité always rose at first light to make sure she was in time for mass, and then worked without a break until the evening. As soon as dinner was finished, the crockery cleared away and the door firmly bolted, she would cover the log fire with ashes and go to sleep in front of the fireplace, holding her rosary in her hand. No one could have been more persistent when it came to haggling over prices and, as for cleanliness, the spotless state of her saucepans was the despair of all the other serving maids in Pont-l'Evêque. She wasted nothing and ate slowly, gathering every crumb of her loaf from the table with her fingers, a twelve-pound loaf baked especially for her and which lasted her twenty days.

In all weathers she wore a printed kerchief fastened behind with a pin, a bonnet which completely covered her hair, grey stockings, a red skirt and over her jacket a bibbed apron like those worn by hospital nurses.

Her face was thin and her voice was shrill. At twenty-five, people took her to be as old as forty. After her fiftieth birthday, it became impossible to say what age she was at all. She hardly ever spoke, and her upright stance and deliberate movements gave her the appearance of a woman made out of wood, driven as if by clockwork.

2

Like other girls, she had once fallen in love.

Her father, a stonemason by trade, had been killed falling from some scaffolding. Following this, her mother died and her sisters went their separate ways. A farmer took her in and, even though she was still a very young girl, he would send her out into the fields to look after the cows. She was dressed in mere rags, she shivered with cold and would lie flat on her stomach to drink water from ponds. She was regularly beaten for no reason at all and was eventually turned out of the house for having stolen thirty sous,[5] a theft of which she was quite innocent. She was taken on at another farm, where she looked after the poultry and, because she was well liked by her employers, her friends were jealous of her.

One evening in August (she was eighteen at the time), she was taken to the village fête at Colleville. She was instantly overcome, bewildered by the boisterous sounds of the fiddle music, the lamps in the trees, the array of brightly coloured clothes, the gold crosses and the lace, all those people moving as one in time to the tune. She was standing on her own, shyly, when a young man, fairly well off to judge by his appearance and who had been leaning against the shaft of a farm wagon smoking his pipe, approached her and asked her to dance. He bought her a glass of cider, a cup of coffee, a cake and a silk scarf and, imagining that she understood his motive, offered to accompany her back home. As they were walking along the edge of a field of oats, he thrust her to the ground. She was terrified and began to scream. He ran off.

One evening a little later, she was walking along the road leading to Beaumont and was trying to get past a large hay wagon as it lumbered slowly along. As she was edging her way round the wheels, she recognized Théodore.

He looked at her quite unabashed and said she should forgive his behaviour of the other night; he 'had just had too much to drink'.

She did not know how to answer him and wanted to run away.

He immediately began to talk about the harvest and various important people in the district and told her that his father had left Colleville and bought a farm at Les Ecots, which meant that they were now neighbours. 'Oh, are we!' she said. He said that his parents wanted him to settle down but that he was in no rush and preferred to wait until the right woman came along before he married. She lowered her eyes. He then asked her if she was thinking of marrying. She smiled and said that he was wrong to tease her. 'But I am not teasing you, I swear,' he said, and slipped his left arm around her waist. She walked on with his arm still around her. They were now walking more slowly. There was a gentle breeze, the stars were shining, the huge wagon-load of hay swayed from side to side in front of them and dust rose from the feet of the four horses as they plodded along. Then, without any word of command, the horses turned off to the right. He kissed her once more and she vanished into the darkness.

The following week, Théodore persuaded her to go out with him on several other occasions.

They would meet in a corner of some farmyard, behind a wall or beneath a solitary tree. Félicité was not naive like other young girls of her age; working with the farm animals had taught her a great deal. However, her natural discretion and an intuitive sense of honour prevented her from giving in to Théodore's demands. Théodore found this resistance so frustrating that, in order to satisfy his passion (or maybe out of sheer simple-mindedness), he proposed to her. She was not sure whether to believe him or not, but he insisted that he was serious.

He then announced something rather disturbing: a year ago his parents had paid for someone else to do his military service[6] but he might still be called up at any time. The prospect of serving in the army terrified him. Félicité took this cowardice as a sign of his affection for her and it made her love him all the more. She would slip out of the house at night to meet Théodore, who assailed her with his fears and entreaties.

Eventually, he declared that he would go to the Préfecture[7] himself and find out what the situation was. He would come back and tell Félicité the following Sunday, between eleven o'clock and midnight.

At the appointed time, Félicité ran to meet her lover.

But instead of Théodore, it was one of his friends who stood waiting to meet her.

He informed her that she would never see Théodore again. In order to make sure he could not be called up, he had married a wealthy old lady from Toucques, by the name of Madame Lehoussais.

Félicité's distress was unbounded. She threw herself to the ground, weeping and wailing; she implored God to come to her aid and lay moaning, all alone in the fields, until daylight. Then she made her way back to the farm and announced that she had decided to leave. At the end of the month, having received her wages, she wrapped her few belongings in a shawl and left for Pont-l'Evêque.

Outside the inn she spoke to a woman wearing a widow's hood who, as it happened, was looking for a cook. The young girl knew precious little about cooking but she seemed so willing and so ready to oblige that Madame Aubain eventually said: 'Very well, you may work for me.'

A quarter of an hour later, Félicité was installed in her house.

At first she lived in a constant state of trepidation as a result of 'the sort of house it was' and the memory of 'Monsieur' which seemed to hover over everything! Paul and Virginie,[8] one aged seven and the other barely four, seemed made of some precious material; she liked to give them piggyback rides and was mortified when Madame Aubain instructed her not to keep kissing them. Even so, she was happy. Her new surroundings were very pleasant and her earlier unhappiness quickly faded.

Every Thursday, a group of Madame Aubain's friends came to play Boston.[9] Félicité would set out the cards and the foot-warmers in readiness. The guests always arrived punctually at eight and left as the clock struck eleven.

On Monday mornings, the secondhand dealer who had a shop at the end of the lane would spread his various bits and pieces of ironmongery out on the pavement. The town would be filled with the buzz of voices, with the sounds of horses neighing, lambs bleating, pigs grunting and carts rattling through the streets. At about midday, just when the market was at its busiest, an old peasant would present himself on Madame Aubain's front doorstep – a tall man with a hooked nose and with his hat perched on the back of his head. This was Robelin, the farmer from Geffosses. He would be followed shortly afterwards by Liébard, the farmer from Toucques, short, fat and red in the face, wearing a grey jacket and leather gaiters complete with spurs.

They would both come bearing chickens or cheeses which they hoped they might persuade their landlady to buy. But Félicité was more than a match for their banter and they always respected her for this.

Madame Aubain also received sporadic visits from the Marquis de Grémanville, an uncle of hers who had squandered his money in loose living and who now lived at Falaise on the last bit of property he could still call his own. He would always turn up at lunch time with a loathsome little poodle which left its muddy paw marks all over the furniture. Despite his efforts to behave like a gentleman, raising his hat every time he mentioned his 'late father', habit would soon get the better of him and he would pour himself glass after glass and start telling bawdy jokes. Félicité would politely show him to the door. 'I think you have had enough for today, Monsieur de Grémanville! Do come and see us again soon!' And she would close the door behind him.

But she was always delighted to welcome Monsieur Bourais, a retired solicitor. His white cravat and bald head, the flounces on his shirt-front and the generous cut of his brown frock-coat, the special way he had of bending his arm when taking snuff, indeed everything about his person prompted in Félicité the sort of agitation we always feel when in the presence of some great man.

He looked after the management of 'Madame's' properties

and would shut himself away with her for hours on end in 'Monsieur's' study. He lived in constant fear for his own reputation, had an inordinate respect for the judiciary and claimed to know some Latin.

Thinking that it would help the children to derive some enjoyment from their studies, he bought them an illustrated geography book. It depicted scenes from different parts of the world, cannibals wearing feathered head-dresses, a monkey abducting a young girl, a group of Bedouins in the desert, a whale being harpooned, and so on.

Paul carefully explained all these pictures to Félicité. In fact, this was the only time anyone ever taught her how to read a book.

The children received their lessons from Guyot, a rather pitiful character who worked at the Town Hall, who was noted for his fine handwriting and who used to sharpen his penknife on the sole of his shoe.

Whenever the weather was fine, the whole family would get up early and spend the day at the farm at Geffosses.

The farmyard there was on a slope, with the farmhouse in the middle. One could just see the sea, a little streak of grey in the distance.

Félicité would take a few slices of cold meat from her basket and they would eat in a room adjoining the dairy. This room was all that now remained of a country house which had fallen into ruin. The paper hung in strips from the wall and fluttered in the draught. Madame Aubain sat with her head bowed, absorbed in her memories, the children hardly daring to speak. 'Off you go and play,' she would say. And off they went.

Paul would climb up into the barn, catch birds, play ducks and drakes on the pond or bang the great farm barrels with a stick to make them boom like drums.

Virginie would go and feed the rabbits or run off across the fields gathering cornflowers, showing her dainty embroidered knickers as she ran.

One evening in autumn, they were coming back through the fields.

The moon, which was in its first quarter, lit up part of the sky, and a mist drifted like a scarf over the windings of the river Toucques. A group of cattle, lying in the middle of a field, lazily watched them go by. When they came to the third field, a few of them got to their feet and stood in a circle in front of them. 'There's nothing to be frightened of!' said Félicité and, humming a wistful little tune as she approached, she went up to the nearest of the animals and patted it on the back. It turned away and the others did the same. But no sooner had they got through the next field when they heard a terrifying bellowing. It was a bull that had been hidden by the mist. It began to come towards the two women. Madame Aubain wanted to run. 'No, no, we must not move too quickly!' said Félicité. They walked more quickly, even so, and could hear the bull's loud breathing getting nearer behind them and the pounding of its hoofs on the grass. They knew it was now galloping towards them! Félicité turned round to face it, grabbed clods of earth from the ground and flung them into the bull's face. It lowered its muzzle, shook its horns and began to shudder and bellow with rage. Madame Aubain had now reached the edge of the field with the two children and was frantically trying to find a way of getting over the hedge. Félicité was still steadily retreating before the bull, throwing lumps of turf into its eyes and calling out, 'Hurry up! Hurry up!'

Madame Aubain got down into the ditch, pushing first Virginie and then Paul in front of her. She fell several times as she tried to climb the bank and at last, by dint of sheer determination, she succeeded.

The bull had driven Félicité up against a gate and was blowing slaver into her face. A second later and it would have gored her. In the nick of time she managed to squeeze herself between two bars in the gate. The huge animal was taken completely by surprise and stopped in its tracks.

People in Pont-l'Evêque talked about this adventure for years afterwards. But Félicité never boasted about it and hardly seemed to realize that she had done anything heroic.

Virginie commanded all her attention. The frightening experience with the bull had affected her nerves and Monsieur Poupart, the doctor, recommended sea bathing at Trouville.[10]

In those days, very few people visited the resort. Madame Aubain made enquiries, sought the advice of Bourais and made preparations as if for a long journey.

The day before they left, the luggage was sent off in Liébard's farm wagon. The next day he returned with two horses. One of them had a woman's saddle with a velvet backrest and the other had a cloak rolled up across its back as a makeshift seat. Madame Aubain sat on this behind Liébard. Félicité looked after Virginie on the other horse and Paul rode separately on Monsieur Lechaptois's donkey, which had been lent on the clear understanding that they took great care of it.

The road was so bad that the five-mile journey took them two hours. The horses sank up to their pasterns in the mud and lurched forward in order to pull themselves free. They lost their footing in the ruts and sometimes had to jump. At certain points on the road, Liébard's mare would suddenly stop dead. Liébard would wait patiently for her to move forward again. As they rode on, he would tell them stories about the people who lived along the way, always adding a few personal comments of his own for good measure. In the town centre of Toucques, for instance, as they were passing alongside a house with nasturtiums growing around the windows, he said, with a shrug of his shoulders, 'There's a Madame Lehoussais lives there and, rather than take a young man . . .' Félicité did not hear the rest, for the horses had broken into a trot and the donkey had run on ahead. They turned down a track, a gate swung open, two young farmhands appeared and they all dismounted beside the manure-heap right outside the front door of the farmhouse.

Old Madame Liébard greeted her mistress with effusive expressions of delight. For lunch she served a sirloin of beef, along with tripe, black pudding, a fricassee of chicken, sparkling cider, a fruit tart and plums in brandy, all accompanied by a stream of compliments to Madame who seemed 'in much better health', to Mademoiselle who had grown up into such 'a fine looking young woman', to Monsieur Paul who was such a 'strapping' young man, not forgetting their dear departed grandparents whom the Liébards had known personally, having been in service to the family for several generations. The farm,

like the Liébards themselves, had an old-world feel to it. The
beams in the ceiling were pitted with woodworm, the walls
blackened with smoke, the window panes grey with dust. There
was an oak dresser, cluttered with all manner of implements –
jugs, plates, pewter bowls, wolf-traps, shears for the sheep and
a huge syringe which particularly amused the children. In the
three yards outside, there was not a single tree which did not
have mushrooms growing at its foot or clumps of mistletoe in
its branches. Several had been blown down by the wind but had
begun to grow again where the trunk had been split and all of
them were bent beneath the weight of apples. The thatched roofs
looked like brown velvet of unequal thickness and weathered the
fiercest winds. But the shed for the carts was falling down.
Madame Aubain said that she would arrange to have it repaired
and asked for the horses to be reharnessed.

It took them another half-hour to reach Trouville. The little
caravan had to dismount when they came to the Ecores, a cliff
which jutted out over the boats below. Three minutes later they
had arrived at the end of the quay and turned into the courtyard
of the Golden Lamb, an inn run by old Madame David.

Virginie very quickly began to recover her strength as a result
of the change of air and of bathing in the sea. She did not have
a bathing costume and so she went into the water wearing a
chemise. Afterwards, her maid would help her to get dressed in
a customs officer's hut that was also used by the bathers.

In the afternoon, they would take the donkey and walk out
beyond the Roches-Noires, towards Hennequeville. At first the
path wound up between gently rolling meadows like the lawn
in a park and then came to a plateau where there were grazing
pastures and ploughed fields. The path was lined by holly bushes
which grew amongst the tangle of brambles, and here and there
the branches of a large dead tree traced their zigzag patterns
against the blue of the sky.

There was one particular field in which they usually stopped
to rest themselves, looking down towards Deauville to their left,
Le Havre to their right and, in front of them, the open sea. It lay
shimmering in the sunshine, as smooth as the surface of a mirror
and so calm that they could barely hear the murmur of the

waves. Sparrows twittered from somewhere nearby and the
great dome of the sky lay spread out above them. Madame
Aubain would sit with her needlework, Virginie would sit beside
her, plaiting rushes, Félicité gathered bunches of wild lavender
and Paul, utterly bored, would always be itching to move on.

At other times they would take the ferry across the Toucques
and go looking for shells. At low tide, sea urchins, ormers and
jellyfish were left behind on the sand. The children would chase
after flecks of foam blown about by the breeze. The waves broke
lazily on the sand from one end of the beach to the other. The
beach stretched as far as the eye could see but was bounded on
the landward side by sand dunes which separated it from the
Marais, a broad meadow in the shape of a racecourse. As they
walked back through it towards Trouville, which lay at the foot
of the hill, the town appeared to grow bigger at every step they
took and, with its motley assortment of houses, it seemed to
blossom like a flower garden in colourful disarray.

When it was too hot, they kept to their room. The dazzling
brightness outside cast bars of light through the slats in the
window blinds. There was not a sound to be heard in the village.
Not a soul ventured out into the streets. The prevailing quiet
made everything seem all the more peaceful. From far away
came the sound of the caulkers' hammers beating against the
hull of a boat and the smell of tar was wafted to them on the
listless breeze.

The most exciting event of the day was when the fishing boats
came in. Once past the entrance buoys, they would begin to
tack from side to side. Their main sails would be lowered to
half-mast and, with their foresail swollen like a great balloon,
they would come gliding through the splashing waves right into
the middle of the harbour and suddenly drop anchor. The boat
would then be brought alongside the quay. The sailors would
hoist their fish ashore, still live and quivering. A line of carts
was ready waiting and women in cotton bonnets rushed forward
to take the baskets and to kiss their menfolk.

One day one of these women came up to Félicité. A moment
or two later, Félicité was back in the room at the inn, beside
herself with excitement. She had found one of her lost sisters,

and into the room walked Nastasie Barette, now Leroux, with a baby at her breast, another child holding her right hand and, on her left, a little ship's boy with his hands on his hips and his beret over one ear.

After a quarter of an hour, Madame Aubain asked her to leave.

But after that there was no getting away from them. They would wait just outside the kitchen or follow them when they went for walks. The husband always kept well out of sight.

Félicité became very attached to them. She bought them a blanket, some shirts and a cooking stove. They were obviously out to take advantage of her. Madame Aubain was annoyed that Félicité was not more firm with them. She also took objection to the familiar way in which the nephew spoke to Paul. So, because Virginie had developed a cough and the weather had taken a turn for the worse, she returned to Pont-l'Evêque.

Monsieur Bourais offered his advice on choosing a good school for Paul. The one at Caen was generally considered to be the best. So Paul was sent away to Caen. He said his goodbyes bravely, really quite pleased that he was going to live somewhere where he would have some friends of his own.

Madame Aubain resigned herself to her son going away, knowing that he must have a good education. Virginie quickly got used to being on her own, but Félicité found the house very quiet without him. Soon, however, she had something else to occupy her mind. From Christmas onwards she had to take Virginie to catechism[11] every day.

3

Genuflecting as she went in through the door, Félicité walked up the aisle beneath the high ceiling of the nave, opened the door of Madame Aubain's pew, sat herself down and looked all around her.

The children were seated in the choir stalls, the boys on the right and the girls on the left. The priest stood in front of them beside the lectern. One of the stained-glass windows in the apse showed the Holy Spirit looking down on the Virgin Mary. In

another, the Virgin knelt before the infant Jesus and behind
the tabernacle there was a carving in wood representing Saint
Michael slaying the dragon.

The priest began with a summary of the Holy Scriptures.
Félicité's mind was filled with images of Paradise, the Flood, the
Tower of Babel, cities consumed by flames, peoples dying and
idols cast down. This dazzling recital of events instilled in her a
wholesome respect for the Almighty and a profound fear of his
wrath. She wept at the story of Christ's Passion. Why had they
crucified a man who was so kind to children, fed the hungry,
gave sight to the blind, and who had chosen, out of his own
gentle nature, to be born amongst the poor on the rough straw
of a stable? Seed-time and harvest, the fruits of the vine, all
those familiar things mentioned in the gospels had their place
in her life too. They now seemed sanctified by contact with God.
Félicité loved lambs all the more because of her love for the
Lamb of God, and doves now reminded her of the Holy Spirit.

She found it difficult to imagine what the Holy Spirit actually
looked like because he was not only a bird but sometimes a fire
and sometimes a breath. Perhaps it was the light of the Holy
Spirit that she would see at night-time, flickering at the edge of
the marshes, or his breath which drove the clouds across the
sky, or his voice which made the church bells ring so beautifully.
She sat rapt in adoration of these wonders, delighting in the
coolness of the stone walls and the peacefulness of the church.

Of church dogma she understood not a word and did not
even attempt to understand it. As the curé stood explaining it
all to the children and the children repeated what they had
learnt, Félicité would drop off to sleep, to be woken suddenly
by the clatter of wooden shoes on the stone floor as the children
left the church. And so Félicité came to learn her catechism by
dint of hearing the children recite it, for her own religious
education had been neglected when she was young. From then
on, she copied the religious observances of Virginie, fasting
when she fasted and going to confession whenever she did. For
the feast of Corpus Christi, Félicité and Virginie made an altar
of repose[12] together.

For days beforehand, Félicité fretted over the preparations

for Virginie's first communion. She worried about her shoes, her rosary, her missal and her gloves. Her hands trembled as she helped Madame Aubain to dress her.

All through the mass she was on tenterhooks. One half of the choir stalls was hidden from her sight by Monsieur Bourais, but straight in front of her she could see the flock of young girls all wearing white crowns over their lowered veils and looking like a field of snow. Even from a distance, she could recognize her beloved little Virginie by the delicate line of her neck and her attitude of reverent contemplation. The bell tinkled. They all bowed their heads and knelt in silence. Then, with a mighty flourish from the organ, the choir and congregation sang the *Agnus Dei*. After the boys had processed forwards, the girls stood up. With their hands joined in prayer, they moved slowly towards the candle-lit altar, knelt at the altar-step, received the Host one by one and returned in the same order to their place in the choir stalls. When it came to Virginie's turn, Félicité leant further forwards so that she could see her and, with that singular imagination that is born of true love, she felt she was herself Virginie, assuming her expression, wearing her dress and with her heart beating inside her breast. As Virginie opened her mouth, Félicité closed her eyes and almost fainted.

The next morning, bright and early, Félicité went to the sacristy and asked to be given communion. She received it with due reverence but did not experience the same rapture.

Madame Aubain wanted the best possible education for her daughter and, because Guyot was unable to teach her either English or music, she resolved to send her to the Ursuline convent school in Honfleur.[13]

Virginie had no objection to this plan but Félicité was most unhappy and felt that Madame was being too strict. However, she came to accept that it was not really for her to decide and that her mistress probably knew best.

Then one day, an old carriage drew up outside the door. Out of it got a nun who had come to collect Mademoiselle. Félicité loaded the luggage up on to the rack, issued some parting instructions to the driver and put six pots of jam, a dozen pears and a bunch of violets in the boot.

Just as they were about to leave, Virginie burst into tears. She clung to her mother, who kissed her on the forehead and kept telling her: 'Come, come, we must be brave!' The step was pulled up and the carriage drove away.

When it had gone, Madame Aubain broke down and that evening all her friends, Monsieur and Madame Lormeau, Madame Lechaptois, the two Rochefeuille sisters, Monsieur de Houppeville and Bourais, came round to comfort her.

At first, the loss of her daughter left her feeling very sad. But she received letters from her on three days each week and on the other days she wrote back to her, walked in her garden, read a little and so managed to occupy her time.

Every morning, out of habit, Félicité would go into Virginie's bedroom and gaze at the walls. She missed being able to comb her hair for her, tie her bootlaces and tuck her up in bed; she missed seeing her sweet little face always beside her and holding her hand when they went out for walks. For want of something to do, she tried to take up lace work. But she was too clumsy with her fingers and she kept breaking the threads. She could not put her mind to anything and was losing sleep. She was, in her own words, 'all empty inside'.

In order to provide herself with 'a bit of company', she asked Madame Aubain if her nephew Victor might be allowed to visit her.

He would always arrive on Sundays, just after mass, rosy-cheeked, his shirt unbuttoned and bringing with him the smells of the countryside through which he had travelled. She straight away laid the table for him. They would eat lunch sitting opposite each other, Félicité taking care to eat as little as possible so as to save on expense and giving Victor so much to eat that he ended up falling asleep. As the first bell for vespers began to ring, she would wake him up, give his trousers a good brush, tie his tie, and make her way to church, leaning on his arm like a proud mother.

His parents always told him to make sure he brought something back with him, a bag of sugar, a piece of soap, a little brandy or even money. He brought with him any of his clothes that needed mending and Félicité always did the work willingly, glad of any opportunity of encouraging him to visit her again.

In August, Victor went to join his father on his sea trips along the coast.

It was the beginning of the school holidays and it was some consolation to Félicité to have the children back at home. But Paul had become rather temperamental and Virginie was now too grown-up to be treated as a little child, which created a sense of awkwardness and distance between them.

Victor's travels took him to Morlaix, to Dunkirk and to Brighton and after each trip he brought back a present for Félicité. The first was a little box made out of shells, the second a coffee cup and the third a big gingerbread man. He was growing into a handsome young man, with a fine figure, the first signs of a moustache, a frank and open expression and a little leather cap which he wore perched on the back of his head like a sea pilot. He would entertain Félicité by telling her stories laced with all sorts of nautical jargon.

One Monday, 14 July 1819 (it was a date that Félicité was never to forget), Victor announced that he had been signed on to the crew of an ocean-going ship and that in two days' time he would be taking the night ferry from Honfleur to join his schooner, which was due shortly to set sail from Le Havre. He might be away for two years.

The prospect of such a long separation left Félicité feeling very saddened. In order to say one final farewell to him, on the Wednesday evening, after Madame had finished her dinner, she put on her clogs and ran the ten miles from Pont-l'Evêque to Honfleur.

When she came to the Calvary,[14] instead of turning left, she turned right, got lost in the shipyards and had to retrace her steps. She asked directions from some passers-by, who told her she would have to hurry. She walked all the way round the harbour, which was full of boats, getting caught up in the moorings as she went. Suddenly the ground seemed to fall away beneath her, beams of light criss-crossed before her eyes and she thought she must be losing her senses when she saw some horses in the sky overhead.

On the quayside, more horses were neighing, frightened by

the sea. They were being hoisted into the air by a derrick and
then lowered into a boat which was already crammed with
passengers trying to squeeze their way between barrels of cider,
baskets of cheese and sacks of grain. Hens were cackling and
the captain was swearing. One of the deck-hands, apparently
oblivious to everything around him, stood leaning against the
cat-head. Félicité had not recognized him and was calling out
'Victor!' again and again. He looked up and she rushed forward,
but just at that moment the gangway was suddenly pulled
ashore.

The boat moved out of the harbour, hauled along by a group
of women who sang in chorus as they went about their work.
Its ribs creaked and heavy waves lashed its bows. The sail swung
round and hid everyone from view. The surface of the sea shone
like silver in the moonlight and on it the ship appeared as a
black spot, growing paler as it moved away. Eventually it was
swallowed up in the distance and vanished from sight.

Returning home, Félicité passed by the Calvary and was taken
by a sudden desire to commend to God's mercy all that she held
dear. She stood there praying for a long time, with tears running
down her cheeks and her eyes fixed on the clouds above. The
town was fast asleep; the only people about were the customs
men. Water could be heard gushing through the holes in the
lock-gate like a running torrent. A clock struck two.

The convent would not be open to visitors before daybreak
and Félicité knew that, if she arrived back late, Madame was
sure to be annoyed. So, although she would have loved just one
small kiss from Virginie, she set off back home. The maids at
the inn were just waking up as she walked into Pont-l'Evêque.

So poor little Victor was to spend months on end being tossed
around on the waves! His previous trips at sea had not bothered
her. England and Brittany were places one came back from.
But America, the colonies and the Antilles were lost in some
unknown region on the other side of the world.

From the day he left, Félicité could not stop thinking about
her nephew. When it was hot and sunny, she worried that he
might be thirsty and when there was a storm, she feared he
might be struck by lightning. As she listened to the wind howling

in the chimney and blowing slates off the roof, she pictured him buffeted by the same storm, clinging to the top of a broken mast and being flung backwards into a sheet of foam. At other times, prompted by her recollection of the pictures in the geography book, she imagined him being eaten by savages, captured by monkeys in a forest or dying on some deserted beach. But she never spoke about these worries to anyone.

Madame Aubain had worries of her own about her daughter. The sisters at the convent said that she was an affectionate child, but over-sensitive. The slightest emotion unsettled her and she had to give up playing the piano.

Her mother insisted that she wrote home regularly. One morning, when the postman had failed to appear, she could scarcely contain her impatience and kept pacing backwards and forwards in her room between her armchair and the window. This really was extraordinary! No news for four days!

Thinking that her own situation might serve as some comfort to her mistress, Félicité ventured:

'But Madame, I haven't received any news for six months!'

'News from whom?'

'Why, news from my nephew,' Félicité gently replied.

'Oh, your nephew!' And with a shrug of her shoulders, Madame Aubain began pacing about the room again, as if to say, 'I hadn't given him a thought! And in any case, he's no concern of mine! A mere ship's boy, a scrounger; he's not worth bothering about! But someone like my daughter . . . Really!'

Although Félicité had been fed such rough treatment since she was a child, she felt very offended by Madame Aubain. But she soon got over it.

After all, it was to be expected that Madame should get upset about her own daughter.

For Félicité, the two children were of equal importance; they were bound together by her love for them and it seemed right that they should share the same fate.

Félicité learnt from the chemist that Victor's ship had arrived in Havana. He had read the announcement in a newspaper.

Because of its association with cigars, Félicité imagined

Havana to be a place in which the only thing people did was
to smoke and she pictured Victor walking amongst crowds
of Negroes in a cloud of tobacco smoke. Was it possible to
return from Havana by land, 'if need be'? How far was it
from Pont-l'Evêque? In order to find out, she went to consult
Monsieur Bourais.

He reached for his atlas and launched into a disquisition on
lines of longitude. Félicité was utterly bewildered. Bourais sat
in front of her, beaming smugly to himself, like the know-all he
was. Eventually, he picked up his pencil and pointed to an
almost invisible black dot in one of the little indentations in the
contour of an oval-shaped patch on the map. 'Here it is,' he
said. Félicité peered closely at the map. The network of coloured
lines was a strain on her eyes, but it told her nothing. Bourais
asked her what was puzzling her and she asked him if he would
show her the house in which Victor was living. Bourais raised
his arms in the air, sneezed and roared with laughter, delighted
to come across someone so simple-minded. Félicité, whose
understanding was so limited that she probably even expected
to see a picture of her nephew, could not understand what he
found so funny.

It was a fortnight after this, at his usual time on market day,
that Liébard came into the kitchen and handed Félicité a letter
which he had received from her brother-in-law. As neither of
them could read, Félicité showed the letter to her mistress.

Madame Aubain, who was counting the stitches on a piece of
knitting, put her work to one side, opened the letter, gave a
sudden start and then, lowering her voice and looking very
serious, she said, 'They are sending you . . . bad news. Your
nephew . . .'

Victor was dead. That was all the letter said.

Félicité sank down on to a chair and leant her head against
the wall. Her eyelids closed and suddenly flushed pink. She
remained there, her head bowed, her hands hanging limply at
her side, staring in front of her and repeating over and over
again, 'The poor boy! The poor boy!'

Liébard stood looking at her and sighing. Madame Aubain
was shaking slightly.

She suggested that Félicité might go and see her sister at Trouville.

Félicité gave a wave of her hand to indicate that it was not necessary.

There was a silence. Old Liébard thought it best to leave.

When he had gone, Félicité said, 'It doesn't matter a bit, not to them it doesn't.'

She lowered her head again and sat there, now and then toying distractedly with the knitting needles that lay on the work-table.

A group of women passed by in the yard, wheeling a barrow-load of dripping linen.

Félicité caught sight of them through the window and suddenly remembered that she had washing to do herself. She had passed the lye[15] through it the day before and today it needed rinsing. She got up and left the room.

Her washing board and her tub were on the bank of the Toucques. She flung her pile of chemises on to the ground beside the river, rolled up her sleeves and seized her battledore. The drubbing could be heard in all the neighbouring gardens. The fields lay deserted and the wind rippled the surface of the river. On the river-bed, long strands of weed drifted with the current, like the hair of corpses floating downstream in the water. Félicité managed to restrain her grief and was very brave until the evening, but when she was alone in her room she gave in to it, lying prone on her mattress with her face buried in the pillow and pressing her fists to her temples.

Much later, she came to learn the circumstances of Victor's death from the captain of his ship. He had caught yellow fever and had been bled too much in the hospital. Four separate doctors had given him the same treatment and he had died immediately. The chief doctor's comment was, 'Good, that's one more to add to the list!'

Victor had always been treated cruelly by his parents and Félicité preferred not to see them again. They did not get in touch with Félicité either; perhaps they had simply forgotten about her or perhaps poverty had hardened their hearts.

Virginie was now growing weaker.

Difficulty in breathing, a persistent cough, a constant high temperature and pale blotches on her cheeks all pointed to some underlying disorder. Monsieur Poupart had advised a holiday in Provence. Madame Aubain decided to follow his advice and would have brought Virginie back home immediately, had it not been for the weather at Pont-l'Evêque.

She had a standing arrangement with a job-master,[16] who drove her to the convent every Tuesday. In the convent garden there was a terrace overlooking the Seine where Virginie would walk up and down over the fallen vine leaves, leaning on her mother's arm. She would look out at the sails in the distance and the whole sweep of the estuary from the chateau at Tancarville to the lighthouses at Le Havre. Sometimes the sun would suddenly break through the clouds and make her blink. Afterwards, they would rest under the arbour. Her mother had procured a little flask of the choicest Malaga wine, from which Virginie would take just two tiny sips, laughing at the thought of making herself tipsy.

She began to recover her strength. Autumn gradually slipped by. Félicité did all she could to reassure Madame Aubain. But one evening, on her way back from an errand in the town, she noticed Monsieur Poupart's gig standing at the front door. Monsieur Poupart himself was in the entrance hall and Madame Aubain was fastening her bonnet.

'Bring me my foot-warmer, my purse and my gloves! Hurry!'

Virginie had pneumonia and Madame feared she was beyond recovery.

'I'm sure it's not that bad,' said the doctor, and the two of them climbed into his carriage, with the snowflakes falling in great flurries around them. Night was drawing on and it was bitterly cold.

Félicité dashed into the church to light a candle and then began to run after Monsieur Poupart's gig. It was a full hour before she caught up with it. She jumped up behind it and clung to the fringe. Suddenly a thought occurred to her. 'The gate to the courtyard was not locked! What if thieves should break in!' She jumped back down on to the road.

The next day, at the very first sign of daylight, she went to the doctor's house. The doctor had returned but had already left again to visit patients in the country. She waited at the inn, thinking that someone or other might arrive with a letter. Eventually, in the half-light of morning, she boarded the Lisieux stagecoach.

The convent was situated at the foot of a steep narrow street. When she was about half-way down the street, she began to make out strange sounds coming from the convent; it was the tolling of a death bell. 'It must be for someone else', she thought, and gave the door-knocker a loud rap.

After some considerable time, she heard the shuffle of foot-steps, the door was inched open and a nun appeared.

The good sister solemnly announced that 'she had just passed away'. At precisely the same moment, the bell of Saint-Léonard's began to toll even more strongly.

Félicité went up to the second floor.

She stood in the doorway of the bedroom and could see Virginie laid out on her back, her hands clasped together, her mouth open and her head tilted backwards. Above her head and inclined towards her was a black crucifix; her face was whiter than the drapes which hung stiffly around her. Madame Aubain lay hugging the foot of the bed and sobbing wildly. The Mother Superior stood beside her on the right. On the chest of drawers, three candlesticks gave out little circles of red light; outside, the fog whitened the window panes. Some nuns came and led Madame Aubain away.

Félicité did not leave Virginie's bedside for two whole nights. She sat there, repeating the same prayers over and over again; she would get up to sprinkle holy water on the sheets, then come back to her chair and continue to gaze fixedly at the dead girl. At the end of her first night's vigil, she noticed that her face was beginning to turn yellow, her lips were turning blue, her nose had grown thinner and her eyes had become sunken. More than once she kissed her eyes and would not have been in the least surprised if Virginie had opened them again; to minds like hers, the supernatural appears perfectly ordinary. She laid her out, wrapped her in her shroud, put her in her coffin, placed a wreath upon her and spread out her hair. Her hair was fair and amazingly long for a girl of her age. Félicité cut off a large lock of it and slipped half of it into her bosom, resolving that it would never be separated from her.

The body was brought back to Pont-l'Evêque, according to Madame Aubain's instructions. Madame Aubain followed the hearse in a closed carriage.

After the funeral mass, it took another three-quarters of an hour to get to the cemetery. Paul led the procession, sobbing. Monsieur Bourais walked behind him, followed in turn by various dignitaries from Pont-l'Evêque, the women, all wearing black veils, and lastly Félicité. Félicité could not help thinking of her nephew and, having been unable to offer him these last honours, she now felt an added grief, as if he were being buried along with Virginie.

Madame Aubain's despair knew no bounds.

At first she rebelled against God, thinking it was unjust that He should take her daughter from her when she had never done any wrong and when there was nothing for her to feel guilty about. But perhaps there was. She should have taken her to the South. Other doctors would have cured her. She blamed herself, wished she could follow her daughter to the grave and called out in anguish in the middle of her dreams. One dream in particular tormented her. Her husband, dressed like a sailor, had returned from a long voyage and, choking back his tears, told her that he had received an order to take Virginie away. They then both racked their brains to think of a hiding place for her.

On one occasion she came in from the garden distraught. Just a moment before (and she pointed to the spot), the father and daughter had appeared in front of her, one after the other. They were not doing anything; they were just staring at her.

For several months she remained in her room, totally listless. Félicité gently admonished her, telling her that she should look after herself for the sake of her son and her late husband and in memory of 'her'.

'Her?' said Madame Aubain as though waking from sleep.

'Oh yes, of course. You haven't forgotten her, have you!' This
was a reference to the cemetery, which Madame Aubain had
been expressly forbidden to visit.

Félicité went there every day.

On the stroke of four, she would walk past the row of houses,
climb the hill, open the gate and approach Virginie's grave.
There was a little column of pink marble standing on a stone
base, with a small garden surrounded by chains. The separate
beds could hardly be seen beneath the covering of flowers.
Félicité would water the leaves, place fresh sand on the garden
and get down on her hands and knees to make sure the ground
was properly weeded. When Madame Aubain was eventually
able to come to see the grave, she found it a source of comfort,
a kind of consolation for her loss.

The years passed, one very much like another, marked only
by the annual recurrence of the church festivals: Easter, the
Assumption, All Saints' Day. It was only little incidents in their
daily lives that, in later years, enabled them to recall a particular
date. Thus in 1825 two glaziers whitewashed the entrance hall;
in 1827 a part of the roof fell into the courtyard and nearly
killed a passer-by. In the summer of 1828 it was Madame's
turn to distribute consecrated bread to the parishioners. This
was also about the same time that Bourais mysteriously left
the town. One by one, all their old acquaintances went away:
Guyot, Liébard, Madame Lechaptois, Robelin and old Uncle
Gremanville, who had been paralysed for many years.

One night, the driver of the mail-coach arrived in Pont-
l'Evêque with news of the July Revolution.[17] A few days later,
a new subprefect was appointed: the Baron de Larsonnière,
who had previously been a consul in America. He arrived in
Pont-l'Evêque accompanied not only by his wife but also by his
sister-in-law and three young girls, all of them already quite
grown up. They were often to be seen on their lawn, dressed in
long, flowing smocks. They also had a Negro servant and a
parrot. They called on Madame Aubain to pay their respects
and she made a point of doing likewise. As soon as she spotted
them approaching in the distance, Félicité would come running
in to tell Madame Aubain that they were on their way. But there

was only one thing that could really awaken her interest and that was her son's letters.

Paul seemed unable to settle down to a career and spent much of his time in the tavern. Madame Aubain would pay off his debts, but he immediately ran up new ones. She would sit at her knitting by the window and heave sighs that Félicité could hear even in the kitchen, where she was working at her spinning wheel.

The two women would often take a stroll together alongside the trellised wall of the garden. They still talked constantly about Virginie, wondering whether she would have liked such and such a thing or trying to imagine what she would have said on such and such an occasion.

All her belongings were still in a cupboard in the children's bedroom. Madame Aubain had avoided looking inside it as much as possible. Then, one summer day, she resigned herself. Moths came flying from the cupboard.

Virginie's frocks hung in a row beneath a shelf upon which there were three dolls, some hoops, a set of doll's furniture and her own hand-basin. The two women took out all the petticoats, stockings and handkerchiefs and spread them out on the two beds before folding them again. This sorry collection of objects lay there, caught in a beam of sunlight which brought out all the stains and the creases that had been made by the movements of Virginie's body. The air was warm, the sky was blue, a blackbird sang outside and the world seemed to be utterly at peace. They found a little chestnut-coloured hat made of long-piled plush, but it had been completely destroyed by the moths. Félicité asked if she might have it as a keepsake. The two women looked at each other and their eyes filled with tears. Madame Aubain opened her arms and Félicité threw herself into them. Mistress and servant embraced each other, uniting their grief in a kiss which made them equal.

It was the first time that this had ever happened, Madame Aubain being, by nature, very reserved. Félicité could not have been more grateful if she had been offered a priceless gift and from then on she doted on her mistress with dog-like fidelity and the reverence that might be accorded to a saint.

As time went by, Félicité's natural kind-heartedness increased.

One day she heard the sound of drums from a regiment marching along the street and she stood at the door with a jug of cider, handing out drinks to the soldiers. She helped to nurse cholera victims and to look after the refugees from Poland. One of the Poles even said he would like to marry her, but they had a serious argument when she came back one morning from the angelus to find him ensconced in her kitchen, calmly helping himself to a salad which she had prepared for lunch.

After the Poles had left, she turned her attention to an old man by the name of Colmiche, who was rumoured to have committed terrible atrocities in '93.[18] He now lived down by the river in a ruined pigsty. The boys in the town used to spy on him through the cracks in the wall and throw stones at him as he lay coughing and choking on his straw bed. He had long, straggling hair, his eyelids were inflamed and on one arm there was a swelling bigger than his head. Félicité provided him with linen and did what she could to keep his hovel clean; she even hoped she might be able to install him in the outhouse, where he would not disturb Madame. When the tumour burst, she changed his dressing every single day. Sometimes she would bring him a small piece of cake or help him outside on to a bundle of straw, where he could lie in the sun. The poor old wretch would splutter and shake and thank her in a barely audible whisper, saying he could not bear to lose her and stretching out his hands the minute he saw her preparing to leave him. He died and Félicité had a mass said for the repose of his soul.

On the same day, she received the most wonderful surprise. Just as she was serving dinner, Madame de Larsonnière's Negro servant arrived, carrying the parrot in its cage, along with its perch, chain and padlock. There was a note from the Baroness, informing Madame Aubain that her husband had been promoted to a Préfecture[19] and that they were leaving Pont-l'Evêque that very evening. She asked Madame Aubain if she would be kind enough to accept the parrot as a memento of their friendship and as a token of her respect.

The parrot had been a source of wonder to Félicité for a long time, for it came from America, a word which always reminded her of Victor. She had already questioned the servant about it and, on one occasion, had even said that 'Madame would be delighted to look after it!'

The Negro had mentioned this to his mistress and, because she could not take it away with her, she readily seized this opportunity of getting it off her hands.

4

The parrot was called Loulou. His body was green, the tips of his wings were pink, the top of his head was blue and his breast was gold-coloured.

Unfortunately, he had the tiresome habit of chewing his perch and he kept plucking out his feathers, scattering his droppings everywhere and splashing the water from his bath all over his cage. He thoroughly irritated Madame Aubain and so she gave him to Félicité to look after.

She decided she would teach him to speak and he was very soon able to say, 'Pretty boy!', 'Your servant, sir!' and 'Hail Mary!' She put him near the front door and a number of visitors were surprised that he would not answer to the name 'Polly', which is what all parrots are supposed to be called. Some people said he looked more like a turkey or called him a blockhead. Félicité found their jibes very hurtful. There was a curious stubborn streak in Loulou which never ceased to amaze Félicité; he would refuse to talk the minute anyone looked at him!

Even so, there was no doubt that he appreciated company. On Sundays, when the Rochefeuille sisters, Monsieur de Houppeville and some of Madame Aubain's new friends – the apothecary Onfroy, Monsieur Varin and Captain Mathieu – came round to play cards, Loulou would beat on the window panes with his wings and make such a furious commotion that no one could hear themselves speak.

He obviously found Bourais's face a source of great amusement. He only had to see it and he would break into fits of uncontrollable laughter. His squawks could be heard echoing round the yard. The neighbours would come to their windows and start laughing too. To avoid being seen by the parrot,

Bourais would slink past the house along the side of the wall, hiding his face behind his hat. He would go down to the river and come into the house by way of the back garden. The looks he gave the bird were not of the tender variety.

The butcher's boy had once flipped Loulou on the ear for trying to help himself to something from his basket and, since then, Loulou always tried to give him a peck through his shirt. Fabu threatened to wring his neck, although he was not cruel by nature, despite what the tattoos on his arms and his long side whiskers might have led one to believe. In fact, he was rather fond of the parrot and, just for the fun of it, he had even tried to teach him a few swear words. Félicité was alarmed at the thought of his acquiring such bad habits and moved him into the kitchen. His chain was removed and he was allowed to wander all over the house.

When he came down the stairs, he would position the curved part of his beak on the step in front of him and then raise first his right foot, followed by his left. Félicité was always worried that these weird acrobatics would make the parrot giddy. He fell ill and could not talk or eat due to an ulcer under his tongue, such as chickens sometimes have. Félicité cured him herself, extracting the lump in his mouth with her fingernails. One day, Monsieur Paul was silly enough to blow cigar smoke up his nose. On another occasion, when Madame Lormeau was teasing him with the end of her parasol, he bit off the metal ferrule with his beak. Then there was the time he got lost.

Félicité had put him out on the grass to get some fresh air. She went indoors for a minute and, when she came back, the parrot had disappeared. She searched for him in the bushes, by the river and even on the rooftops, oblivious to her mistress's shouts of 'Do be careful! You must be mad!' She then hunted through every single garden in Pont-l'Evêque and stopped all the people in the street, asking, 'You don't happen to have seen my parrot by any chance?' Those who did not already know the parrot were given a full description. Suddenly, she thought she saw something green flying about behind the mills at the bottom of the hill. But when she got to the top of the hill, there was nothing to be seen. A pedlar told her he had definitely seen the

bird only a short while ago in old Madame Simon's shop at
Saint-Melaine. Félicité ran all the way there, but nobody knew
what she was talking about. In the end she came back home,
utterly exhausted, her shoes torn to shreds and feeling sick at
heart. She sat down on the middle of the garden bench, next to
Madame, and she was telling her everything that she had done
when she suddenly felt something drop gently on to her shoulder. It was Loulou! What on earth had he been up to? Perhaps
he had just gone for a little walk around the town!

It took Félicité quite a while to recover from this shock. If the
truth were known, she never really recovered from it completely.

She caught tonsillitis, as a result of getting thoroughly chilled,
and shortly afterwards developed pains in her ears. Within three
years she was completely deaf and spoke in a very loud voice,
even in church. Even though her sins could have been proclaimed
in every corner of the diocese without bringing any discredit to
her or causing offence to others, the curé decided that it would
now be best to hear her confession in the sacristy.

Imaginary buzzing noises in her head added to her troubles.
Her mistress would often say, 'Goodness me! You're just being
silly!' Félicité would answer, 'Yes, Madame,' still looking
around her to see where the noises were coming from.

She became enclosed in an ever-diminishing world of her
own; gone for ever was the pealing of church bells and the
lowing of cattle in the fields. Every living thing passed by her in
ghostly silence. Only one sound now reached her ears, and that
was the voice of her parrot.

Almost as if he were deliberately trying to entertain her, he
would imitate the clicking of the turnspit, the shrill cry of the
fishmonger or the sound of sawing from the joiner's shop on
the other side of the street. Whenever the front door bell rang,
he would imitate Madame Aubain: 'Félicité! The door, the
door!'

They would hold conversations with each other, the parrot
endlessly repeating the three stock phrases from his repertory
and Félicité replying with words that made very little sense but
which all came straight from the heart. In her isolation, Loulou
was almost a son to her; she simply doted on him. He used to

climb up her fingers, peck at her lips and hang on to her shawl. Sometimes she would put her face close to his and shake her head in the way a nurse does to a baby, with the wings of her bonnet and the bird's wings all fluttering together.

When storm clouds gathered and thunder rumbled, the bird would squawk loudly, no doubt remembering the sudden cloud-bursts of his native forests. The sound of falling rain would send him into a frenzy. He would fly madly about the house, shooting up to the ceiling, knocking everything over and finally escaping through the window into the garden to splash around in the puddles. But he would soon come back, perch on one of the fire-dogs, jump up and down to dry his feathers and then proudly display his tail or his beak.

One morning in the terrible winter of 1837, when she had put him near the fireplace because of the cold, she found him dead in his cage, hanging head downwards with his claws caught in the metal bars. He had probably died of a stroke, but the thought crossed Félicité's mind that he might have been poisoned with parsley and, although there was no definite proof, her suspicions fell on Fabu.

She wept so much that her mistress eventually said, 'Well, why don't you have him stuffed?'

Félicité went to consult the chemist, who had always been kind to the parrot.

He wrote to Le Havre and a man by the name of Fellacher agreed to do the job. But, knowing that the mail-coach some-times mislaid parcels, Félicité decided that she would take the parrot as far as Honfleur herself.

The road ran between endless lines of apple trees, bare and leafless. Ice lay in the ditches. Dogs barked as she walked past the farms. With her hands tucked under her mantlet and her basket on her arm, Félicité walked briskly along the middle of the road in her little black clogs.

She followed the road through the forest, passed Le Haut-Chêne and eventually reached Saint-Gatien.[20]

On the road behind her, in a cloud of dust and gathering speed on its way down the hill, a mail-coach at full gallop came rushing towards her like a whirlwind. The coachman, seeing that this woman was making no attempt to get out of the way, stood up and looked out over the roof of the carriage and both he and his postilion shouted at her for all their worth. The four horses, which he was vainly trying to rein in, galloped faster and faster towards her and the leading pair struck her as they went by. With a sharp tug on the reins, the coachman forced them to swerve on to the side of the road. In his rage, he raised his arm and lashed out at her with his long whip as the coach lurched past. The blow struck Félicité full across her face and the upper part of her body, and with such force that she fell flat on her back.

The first thing she did when she regained consciousness was to open her basket. Fortunately, Loulou had come to no harm. She felt a burning sensation on her right cheek. She put her hand to her face and saw that her hand was red. She was bleeding.

She sat down on a pile of stones and dabbed her face with her handkerchief. Then she ate a crust of bread which she had brought with her in case she needed it and tried to take her mind off her wound by looking at the parrot.

As she came to the top of the hill at Ecquemauville, she saw the lights of Honfleur twinkling in the night like clusters of stars and, beyond them, the sea, stretching dimly into the distance. She was suddenly overcome with a fit of giddiness and her wretched childhood, the disappointment of her first love affair, the departure of her nephew and the death of Virginie all came flooding back to her like the waves of an incoming tide, welling up inside her and taking her breath away.

She insisted on speaking personally to the captain of the ship and, although she did not tell him what was in her parcel, she asked him to look after it carefully.

Fellacher kept the parrot for a long time. He kept promising that it would arrive the following week. After six months, he announced that a box had been dispatched, but that was the last they heard of it. Félicité began to fear that Loulou would never come back. 'He has been stolen, I know it!' she thought to herself.

But at last he arrived. And quite magnificent he looked too, perched on a branch which was screwed on to a mahogany plinth, with one foot held raised, his head cocked to one side and holding in his beak a nut which the taxidermist, in order to add a little touch of grandeur, had gilded.

Félicité installed him in her room.

This room, which few were allowed into, was filled with a mixture of religious knick-knacks and other miscellaneous bits and pieces and resembled something between a chapel and a bazaar.

A large wardrobe made it awkward to open the door fully. Opposite the window that looked out on to the garden was a smaller circular window which looked out on to the courtyard. There was a plain, unsprung bed and beside it a table with a water jug, two combs and a small cake of blue soap on a chipped plate. Fixed to the walls were rosaries, medals, several pictures of the Virgin and a holy-water stoop made out of a coconut shell. On the chest of drawers, which was draped with a cloth like an altar, was the shell box that Victor had given her, a watering can and a ball, some handwriting books, the illustrated geography book and a pair of little ankle boots. Hanging by its two ribbons from the nail which supported the mirror was the little plush hat! These keepsakes meant so much to Félicité. She had even kept one of Monsieur's frock-coats. If there was anything that Madame Aubain wanted to get rid of, she would find a place for it in her room, like the artificial flowers beside her chest of drawers and the portrait of the Comte d'Artois[21] in the window recess.

Loulou was placed on a little shelf made especially for the purpose and fixed to a chimney breast which protruded into the room. Every morning, as she woke, she would catch sight of him in the early morning light and would recall the days gone by, trivial incidents, right down to the tiniest detail, remembered not in sadness but in perfect tranquillity.

Being unable to hold a conversation with anyone, she lived her life as if in a sleepwalker's trance. The only thing that seemed capable of bringing her back to life was the Corpus Christi procession, when she would visit all the neighbours, collecting candlesticks and mats to decorate the altar of repose that was always set up outside in the street.

When she went to church, she would sit gazing at the picture of the Holy Spirit and it struck her that it looked rather like her parrot. The resemblance was even more striking in an Epinal colour print[22] depicting Our Lord's baptism. The dove had wings of crimson and a body of emerald-green and it looked for all the world like Loulou. Félicité bought the picture and hung it in place of the portrait of the Comte d'Artois, so that she could see them both together at the same time. In her mind, the one became associated with the other, the parrot becoming sanctified by connection with the Holy Spirit and the Holy Spirit in turn acquiring added life and meaning. Surely it could not have been a dove that God had chosen to speak through, since doves cannot talk. It must have been one of Loulou's ancestors. Félicité would say her prayers with her eyes turned towards the picture but every now and then she would turn her head slightly to look at the parrot.

She thought of entering the sisterhood of the Ladies of the Virgin but Madame Aubain persuaded her not to.

There now occurred an event of considerable importance – Paul's wedding.

Having worked first as a lawyer's clerk, Paul had subsequently tried his hand at business, worked for the Customs and for the Inland Revenue and had even considered joining the Department of Forests and Waterways. Now, at the age of thirty-six, as if by divine inspiration, he had suddenly discovered his vocation – the Registry Office![23] Indeed, he had displayed such a talent for the job that one of the inspectors had offered him his daughter's hand in marriage and had promised to use his influence to advance his career.

By now, Paul took his responsibilities seriously and he brought his intended to see his mother.

Not a thing at Pont-l'Evêque met with her approval. She expected to be treated like royalty and she hurt Félicité's feelings badly. Madame Aubain was relieved to see her go.

The following week, they learned of the death of Monsieur Bourais in an inn somewhere in Lower Brittany. Rumour had it that he had committed suicide. This turned out to be true and questions were raised about his honesty. Madame Aubain went through her accounts and the catalogue of his misdeeds soon became apparent: embezzlement of arrears of rent, undeclared sales of wood, forged receipts, and so forth. It was also discovered that he was the father of an illegitimate child and that he was having 'an illicit relationship with someone from Dozulé'.

This sordid business was a source of great distress to Madame Aubain. In March 1853, she began to feel pains in her chest. A grey coating covered her tongue. She was treated with leeches but this failed to improve her breathing. On the ninth evening of her illness, she died, aged just seventy-two.

People took her to be younger than this because of her dark hair, which she had always worn in bandeaux[24] round her pale, pockmarked face. She had very few friends to lament her death; there was a certain haughtiness about her that had always kept people at a distance.

Félicité wept for her in a way that servants rarely weep for their masters. That Madame should die before her disturbed her whole way of thinking; it seemed to go against the natural order of things; it was something unacceptable and unreal.

Ten days later, just as soon as they could get there from Besançon, the heirs arrived on the scene. Madame Aubain's daughter-in-law went through all the drawers, chose a few pieces of furniture for herself and sold what was left. Then they all went back to the Registry Office.

Madame's armchair, her little table, her foot-warmer and the eight chairs had all gone! On the walls, yellow patches marked the places where pictures had once hung. They had taken away the children's beds, along with their mattresses, and the cupboard had been cleared of all Virginie's things. Félicité went from room to room, heartbroken.

The following day, a notice appeared on the front door. The apothecary shouted into Félicité's ear that the house was for sale.

Félicité's head began to swim and she had to sit down.

What most upset her was the thought of having to move out of her own room; it was the perfect place for poor Loulou. In her anguish she would gaze at him and beg the Holy Spirit to come to her aid. She developed the idolatrous habit of kneeling in front of the parrot to say her prayers. Sometimes the sun would catch the parrot's glass eye as it came through the little window, causing an emanation of radiant light that sent her into ecstasies.

Félicité had been left a pension of three hundred and eighty francs[25] by her mistress. The garden provided her with vegetables. As for clothes, she had sufficient to last her her lifetime and she saved on lighting by going to bed as soon as it began to get dark.

She hardly ever went out, because she disliked walking past the secondhand dealer's shop, where some of the old furniture was on display. Ever since her fit of giddiness, she had been dragging one leg and, as she was now growing frail, old Madame Simon, whose grocery business had recently collapsed, used to come round every morning to chop her firewood and draw her water.

Her eyes grew weaker. The shutters were no longer opened. Many years passed. Nobody came to rent the house and nobody came to buy it.

Félicité never asked for any repairs to be done, because she was frightened she might be evicted. The laths in the roof rotted and for one whole winter her bolster was permanently wet from the rain. Shortly after Easter, she coughed blood.

Madame Simon called for a doctor. Félicité wanted to know what was wrong with her. But by now she was too deaf to hear what was said and she only managed to catch one word: 'pneumonia'. It was a word she knew and she quietly answered, 'Ah! Like Madame', finding it quite natural that she should follow in her mistress's footsteps.

The time for preparing the altars of repose was drawing near.

The first of them was always placed at the foot of the hill, the second outside the post office and the third about half-way up the street. The exact position of this last altar was a matter of some rivalry, but the women of the parish eventually agreed that it should be placed in Madame Aubain's courtyard.

Félicité's breathing was getting worse and she was becoming more feverish. She fretted at not being able to do anything for the altar. If only there were at least something that she could put on it! And then she thought of the parrot. The neighbours objected, saying that it was not really suitable. But the curé gave his permission and this made Félicité so happy that she asked him to accept Loulou, the one treasure she possessed, as a gift from her when she died.

From Tuesday to Saturday, the eve of Corpus Christi, her coughing increased. By the evening, her face looked drawn, her lips were sticking to her gums and she began vomiting. The following morning, at first light, feeling very low, she sent for a priest. Three good women stood round her as she was given extreme unction. She then announced that she needed to speak to Fabu.

Fabu arrived dressed in his Sunday best and feeling very ill at ease in such sombre surroundings.

'Please forgive me,' she said, summoning all her strength to extend her arm towards him, 'I thought it was you who had killed him.'

What was all this nonsense? How could she suspect someone like him of having committed a murder! Fabu was most indignant and was on the point of losing his temper.

'Her mind is wandering,' they said. 'Surely you can see that.'

From time to time Félicité seemed to be speaking to phantoms. The women went away. Madame Simon ate her lunch.

A little later she went to fetch Loulou and held him close to Félicité. 'Come on,' she said. 'Say goodbye to him.'

Although Loulou was not a corpse, he was being eaten away by maggots. One of his wings was broken and the stuffing was coming out of his stomach. But Félicité was now blind. She kissed him on his forehead and held him against her cheek. Madame Simon took him from her and went to replace him on the altar.

5

The smells of summer drifted in from the meadows. The air was filled with the buzzing of flies. The sun glinted on the surface of the river and warmed the slates of the roof. Madame Simon had come back into the room and was gently nodding off to sleep.

She was awoken by the sound of bells; they were coming out of vespers. Félicité grew suddenly calmer. She thought of the procession and saw everything as clearly as if she were there.

All the schoolchildren, the choristers and the firemen were walking along the pavements. In the middle of the street, at the head of the procession, came the church officer with his halberd, the beadle carrying the great cross, the schoolmaster in charge of the boys and the nun keeping a motherly eye on the girls. Three of the prettiest, looking like curly headed angels, were throwing rose petals in the air. They were followed by the deacon conducting the band with arms outstretched and two censer-bearers turning round at every step to face the Holy Sacrament, which was carried by Monsieur le Curé,[26] clad in his magnificent chasuble and protected by a canopy of bright red velvet held aloft by four churchwardens. A great throng of people followed on behind as the procession made its way between the white sheets which draped the walls of the houses and eventually arrived at the bottom of the hill.

Félicité's forehead was bathed in a cold sweat. Madame Simon sponged it with a cloth, telling herself that one day she would go the same way.

The noise of the crowd gradually increased, at one point becoming very loud and then fading away.

A sudden burst of gunfire rattled the window panes. The postilions were saluting the monstrance. Félicité rolled her eyes and, trying to raise her voice above a whisper, she asked, 'Is he all right?' She was still worrying about the parrot.

Félicité was now entering her final moments. Her breath came in short raucous gasps, making her sides heave. Beads of froth gathered in the corners of her mouth and her whole body began to shake.

From the street outside came the blaring of ophicleides,[27] the high-pitched voices of the children and the deeper voices of the men. There were moments when all was quiet and all that could be heard was the tread of feet, cushioned by the scattered petals and sounding like a flock of sheep crossing a field.

The group of clergy entered the courtyard. Madame Simon climbed up on to a chair to look out of the little window and was able to see the altar directly below.

It was hung with green garlands and covered with a flounce in English point lace. Standing in the centre was a little square frame containing some relics and at each end there was an orange tree. Along the length of the altar there was a row of silver candlesticks and china vases containing a vivid display of sunflowers, lilies, peonies, foxgloves and bunches of hydrangea. A cascade of bright colours fell from the top of the altar down to the carpet spread out on the cobblestones beneath it. In amongst the flowers could be seen a number of other treasured ornaments: a silver-gilt sugar-bowl decorated with a ring of violets, a set of pendants cut from Alençon gemstones glittering on a little carpet of moss, two Chinese screens with painted landscapes. Loulou lay hidden beneath some roses and all that could be seen of him was the spot of blue on the top of his head, like a disc of lapis lazuli.

The churchwardens, the choristers and the children took up their places around three sides of the courtyard. The priest slowly walked up the steps and placed his great shining orb on the lace altar cloth. Everyone fell to their knees. There was a deep silence in which all that could be heard was the sound of the censers sliding on their chains as they were swung backwards and forwards.

A blue haze of incense floated up into Félicité's room. She opened her nostrils wide to breathe it in, savouring it with mystical fervour. Her eyes closed and a smile played on her lips. One by one her heartbeats became slower, growing successively weaker and fainter like a fountain running dry, an echo fading away. With her dying breath she imagined she saw a huge parrot hovering above her head as the heavens parted to receive her.

THE LEGEND OF SAINT JULIAN HOSPITATOR

Julian's father and mother lived in a castle in the middle of a forest, on the slope of a hill.

The four towers at the corners had pointed roofs with lead cladding, and the base of the walls was built on outcrops of rock which fell steeply to the bottom of the moat.

The paving in the courtyard was spotlessly clean like the stone floor of a church. Projecting from the roof were gargoyles, in the shape of dragons with their mouths pointing downwards, which spat rainwater into the cistern below. Every window sill from the top to the bottom of the castle carried a painted earthenware flowerpot planted with either basil or heliotrope.

An outer enclosure, surrounded by wooden stakes, contained an orchard of fruit trees, a flower garden with different varieties of plants arranged in patterns, an arbour with covered walks for taking the air and an alley where the pageboys could enjoy a game of mall.[1] In the other half of this enclosure were the kennels, the stables, the bakery, the winepress and the barns. Surrounding it all was a lush green meadow, which was itself enclosed by a thick hedge of thorn.

There had been such a prolonged period of peace that the portcullis could no longer be lowered, grass grew in the moat, swallows made their nests in the loopholes of the battlements and the archer who patrolled the castle walls during the daytime retired to his watchtower the minute the sun became too hot and dropped off to sleep like a monk.

Inside the castle, all the metal fittings gleamed, the bedchambers were hung with tapestries as protection against the cold, the cupboards were crammed with linen, the cellars were piled high with casks of wine and the oak coffers groaned beneath the weight of moneybags.

The walls of the armoury were lined with military trophies and the heads of wild beasts, and in between them were displayed weapons of every age and every nation, from Amalekite slings and Garamantian spears to Saracen brackmards and Norman coats of mail.

The great roasting-spit in the kitchen could carry a whole ox and the chapel was as richly furnished as the oratory of a king. In one secluded corner of the castle there was even a Roman-style bath, but the noble lord refrained from using it, as he considered bathing to be a heathen practice.

He was always to be seen wrapped in a cloak of fox-skin, striding about his domain, dispensing justice to his vassals[2] or settling the disputes of his neighbours. In winter he would sit watching the snowflakes fall or have stories read to him. At the first sign of fine weather, he would ride out on his mule along the lanes beside the ripening corn, talking with the peasants and offering them advice. After many adventures, he had taken as his wife a damsel of noble birth.

She was very fair of skin, rather haughty and demure. As she moved about the castle, the tip of her headdress brushed against the lintel of the doorways and the train of her linen dress stretched three full paces behind her. The running of her household was as carefully regulated as that of a monastery. Every morning she would issue tasks to her servants, supervise the making of jams and ointments, spin at her wheel or embroider altar-cloths. After much praying to God, she bore a son.

This was the occasion of great rejoicing and a feast which lasted for three days and four nights. The castle was lit by torchlight and echoed to the sound of harps. The floors were strewn with greenery. There were the very rarest of spices and fowls as fat as sheep. To everyone's great amusement, out of one of the pies there suddenly popped a dwarf. The crowd of guests grew bigger and bigger until there were no longer enough drinking bowls and they had to drink from hunting horns and helmets.

The young mother did not take part in these festivities and

lay quietly in her bed. One night she woke up and in a shaft of moonlight that came streaming through the window she saw a shadowy figure moving. It was an old man dressed in a rough smock with a rosary hanging at his side and a beggar's scrip slung over his shoulder. Everything about him seemed to suggest he was a hermit. He approached her bed and without opening his lips said:

'Mother, rejoice! Your son is born to be a saint!'

She was about to cry out when, as if he were gliding on the moonbeam, he rose gently into the air and disappeared. The singing from the banquet broke out with renewed vigour. She heard the whisper of angels' voices; her head fell back on to the pillow, over which there hung a martyr's bone set in a frame of garnets.

The next day, the servants were questioned but they all swore that they had not seen a hermit. Whether it were a dream or reality, she was convinced it was a sign from heaven. However, she took care to say nothing about it, lest she be accused of pride.

The guests left at daybreak. Julian's father was standing outside the postern-gate, where he had come to bid farewell to the last of them, when a beggar suddenly appeared out of the morning mist and stood in front of him. He was a gypsy with a plaited beard, silver bangles on his arms and blazing eyes. As if inspired from above, he stammered these incoherent words:

'Ah! Ah! Your son! ... Much bloodshed! ... Much glory! ... Always blessed by fortune! The family of an emperor.'

As he stooped to pick up his alms, he melted into the grass and vanished from sight. The noble lord looked to his right and to his left and called out as loudly as he could. But there was nobody there. All that could be heard was the sighing of the wind as it blew away the morning mists.

He put this vision down to mental fatigue, having had precious little sleep. 'If I tell anyone about it, they will just laugh at me,' he thought. And yet the idea that his son was destined for a life of splendour captivated him, even though the gypsy's prophecy was not clear and he even doubted having heard it.

Both he and his wife kept their secrets from each other. But they continued to dote on their son and, as they now thought of him as someone specially chosen by God, they looked after him with all the care that was possible. His cradle was lined with the finest down; above it was a lamp shaped like a dove, which was kept alight at all times; three nurses rocked him to sleep. To see him snugly wrapped in his swaddling clothes, with his little pink face and blue eyes, his mantle of brocade and his bonnet covered in pearls, he looked like an Infant Jesus. He cut all his teeth without crying once.

When he was seven, his mother taught him to sing. His father sat him on the back of one of his biggest horses to teach him to be brave. The child beamed with delight and wasted no time in finding out everything he possibly could about warhorses.

A learned old monk taught him Holy Scripture, the Arabic numerals, the Latin alphabet and how to paint miniatures on vellum. They would work together at the top of a tower, well away from the noise.

When the lesson was over, they would come back down into the garden and slowly walk round it, studying the flowers as they went.

Sometimes, they would notice a line of packhorses, led by a foot traveller in Eastern dress, wending its way across the valley below. The lord of the castle, recognizing that this was a merchant, would dispatch one of his servants to speak with him. Once persuaded of the lord's good intentions, the traveller would interrupt his journey and come up to the castle. He would be shown into the parlour, and from his chests he would take pieces of velvet and silk, fine jewellery, aromatic spices and other strange objects whose use no one could imagine. Eventually, the fellow would continue on his way, having made a huge profit and having come to no harm. At other times a group of pilgrims would come knocking on the castle door. Their wet clothes would steam in front of the fire. Having eaten their fill, they would tell tales about their travels: voyages on the storm-tossed sea, long treks across burning deserts, fierce encounters with heathens, the deep caves of Syria, the Manger and the Holy Sepulchre. And then they would present the young lord with some of the scallop-shells[3] that they wore on their cloaks.

Often the lord of the castle would entertain his old companions in arms. As they caroused, they would recall the wars they had fought, the attacks on fortresses, the thunder of the siege engines and the terrible wounds of the soldiers. Julian would give cries of delight as he sat listening to these tales, which convinced his father that he was destined to be a great conqueror. But in the evening, as he came out from the angelus and walked between the lines of paupers bowing their heads before him, he would dip into his purse[4] with such modesty and nobility of spirit that his mother felt sure that he would one day become an archbishop.

In chapel, he always sat beside his parents, and, no matter how long the service, he would remain kneeling at his stool with his cap on the floor and his hands joined in prayer.

One day, during mass, as he raised his head, he saw a little white mouse emerge from a hole in the wall. It scampered up on to the first of the altar-steps, ran backwards and forwards a few times and then scurried back into its hole. On the following Sunday, he was disturbed by the thought that he might see the mouse again. Sure enough, the mouse came back. Every Sunday he would wait for it to appear; it irritated him and he came to resent it. He decided that he must get rid of it.

So, having closed the door behind him, he scattered some cake-crumbs on the altar-steps and stationed himself beside the hole with a stick in his hand.

After a very long wait, a little pink snout appeared, followed by the mouse itself. He gave it a quick tap with his stick and was amazed to see its little body lying motionless in front of him. There was a tiny bloodstain on the flagstone. He quickly wiped it clean with his sleeve, threw the mouse outside and said nothing to anyone.

The castle gardens were visited by all manner of fledglings that came to peck at the seeds. Julian devised a method of firing peas from a hollow reed. When he heard birds twittering in a tree, he would tiptoe towards it, take aim with his pipe and blow out his cheeks. The young birds would come showering down on top of him in such great numbers that he could not refrain from laughing out loud, delighted at his own mischief.

One morning, as he was walking back alongside the curtain wall, he saw a fat pigeon preening itself in the sun on top of the battlements. Julian stopped to look at it. There was a breach at this point in the castle wall and he found his hand resting on a chip of loose stone. His arm whisked round, the stone struck the bird and it plummeted into the moat below.

He scrambled down after it, scratching himself on the undergrowth and hunting everywhere with the agility of a young dog.

The pigeon had been caught in the branches of a privet bush; its wings were broken but its body was still quivering.

The child was exasperated by its stubborn refusal to die. He proceeded to wring its neck. The bird's convulsions made his heart beat faster and a flood of savage pleasure ran through his body. As the bird finally went stiff in his hands, he almost swooned.

That evening, as they were eating their supper, his father declared that Julian was now old enough to learn how to hunt and he went off to find an old copybook of his in which every aspect of hunting was explained in a series of questions and answers. In this book, a master demonstrated to his pupil the art of training dogs, taming falcons and setting traps; he explained how to recognize a stag by its droppings, a fox by its footprints or a wolf by the scratch-marks it leaves on the ground, how best to spot their tracks or make them break cover, where an animal is most likely to go to ground and what are the most favourable wind conditions. Finally, there was a list of all the different hunting calls and a set of rules for distributing the kill.

When Julian was able to recite all this by heart, his father presented him with a pack of hunting hounds.

The pack consisted of twenty-four Barbary greyhounds, swifter than gazelles but not always easy to keep to heel, and seventeen pairs of Breton retrievers, their russet coats flecked with white markings, full-chested dogs with an unerring hunting instinct and the most fearsome of barks. For tracking wild boar and for other particularly dangerous confrontations there were forty griffons with coats as shaggy as bears. A group of Tartary mastiffs, as tall as donkeys, the colour of fire, broad-backed and straight-limbed, were specially trained to hunt the wild ox.

There were spaniels with black coats that gleamed like satin and talbots whose bark was as lusty as that of any beagle. In a separate enclosure, growling, shaking their chains and rolling their eyes, were eight Alani wolfhounds, huge beasts capable of savaging a man on horseback and quite fearless even in the face of lions.

All these dogs were fed on the finest wheat bread, drank from special stone water-troughs and each had its own sonorous name.

The falcons were, if anything, even more remarkable than the hounds. The noble lord had spared no expense and had managed to acquire tercel hawks from the Caucasus, sakers from Babylon, gerfalcons from Germany and peregrine falcons captured on high cliffs that brave the icy waters of far distant lands. They were housed in a shed with a thatched roof, each attached to its perch in order of size. In front of the shed was a small expanse of lawn on to which the birds were periodically released in order to give them some exercise.

Rabbit nets, hooks, wolf-traps and all manner of other hunting devices were constructed.

They would often set off into the countryside with a group of pointers. The dogs would quickly mark their prey and the huntsmen would creep forward and carefully spread a huge net over them as they lay motionless on the ground. At a word of command, the dogs would all start barking and flocks of startled quail would fly up into the net. The ladies of the neighbourhood, invited to the hunt by their husbands, the children and the maidservants would all rush forward and the birds were caught with ease.

On other occasions, they would beat a drum to start hares, dig ditches to catch foxes or set traps which would spring shut to catch a wolf by its paw.

But Julian had little taste for such easy contrivances. He much preferred to go off hunting on his own, with just his horse and his falcon. The falcon he chose was nearly always a great Scythian tartaret, as white as snow. Its leather hood was topped with a plume of feathers and golden bells jingled at the tips of its blue feet. It would stand erect on its master's arm as the horse

galloped onwards and the plains unfolded before them. Then
suddenly, Julian would untie its jesses and release the bird into
the air. The bird would soar fearlessly into the sky as straight
as an arrow. Two specks of unequal size would be seen encircling
each other, coming together and then disappearing into the haze
of blue above. The falcon would soon reappear, tearing apart
its prey as it flew back to settle with a flutter of its wings on the
hunter's gauntlet.

In this way, Julian hunted heron, kite, crow and vulture.

He loved to sound his horn and ride along behind his dogs as
they ran down hillsides, leapt across streams and darted back
up into the woods. And when the hunted stag began to moan as
the dogs tore at its flesh, he would quickly dispatch it and then
watch with delight as they frantically devoured the dismembered
carcass, spread out for them on the back of its steaming hide.

When there was a mist, he would hide himself deep in a marsh
and watch for geese, otters and wild duck.

Every morning, three horsemen would be waiting for him at
the foot of the castle steps as soon as it was daylight. The old
monk, looking down from his attic window, would wave his
arms and call him back. But to no avail; Julian never so much
as turned his head. He went off in scorching heat and pouring
rain and even when a storm was blowing. He drank with his
hands from running streams, ate crab apples as he rode along
and rested beneath an oak if he felt weary. He would return
home in the middle of the night, covered in blood and mud, with
thorns caught in his hair and his clothes heavy with the smell of
wild animals. He became like a wild animal himself. Whenever
his mother tried to kiss him, he responded coldly to her embrace
and appeared to be thinking of more important things.

He slew bears with a knife, bulls with a hatchet and wild boar
with a spear. Once, having nothing more than a stick to protect
himself with, he fought off a pack of scavenging wolves that
were gnawing the corpses at the foot of a gibbet.

One winter morning he set out before dawn, well armed, with
a crossbow on his shoulder and a quiver of arrows slung over
his saddle bow.

He was riding a Danish jennet, with two basset hounds following behind; the ground echoed to the sound of its hoofs as he rode steadily along. Little beads of hoar frost clung to his cape; the wind blew strong and chill. The horizon began to brighten to one side of him and in the pale morning light he caught sight of a group of rabbits hopping around outside their burrows. The two basset hounds were upon them in a flash, frantically snatching at them as they scattered and breaking their backs.

Shortly afterwards, he came to a forest. A wood grouse, numbed by the cold, had fallen asleep on the branch of a tree, its head tucked under its wing. With a single backward stroke of his sword, Julian cut off its two feet and then continued on his way without even stopping to retrieve it.

Three hours later, he found himself on a mountain peak, so high that the sky appeared almost black. In front of him a rock face rather like a long wall sloped downwards towards the edge of a deep ravine. At the far end of this wall, two mountain goats stood peering down into the abyss below. Julian did not have his arrows with him, having left his horse behind, and he decided he would climb down the wall in order to get near to them. He approached barefoot and bent almost double and managed to come right up to the first of the two goats. He plunged a dagger between its ribs. The other goat, seized with panic, leapt into the void. Julian lunged forward in order to stab it, but his right foot slipped and he fell on to the dead body of the first goat, with his face looking down into the abyss and his two arms spreadeagled in front of him.

He came back down towards the plain and made his way beside a line of willow trees that grew along the bank of a river. Now and then a crane would swoop down very low above his head. Julian lashed at them with his whip and not one of them escaped his aim.

By now the warmer air had melted the frost, swathes of mist drifted upwards and the sun appeared. In the far distance he saw the glint of a frozen lake, its surface like a sheet of lead. In the middle of the lake stood an animal that Julian did not recognize, a beaver with a black snout. Despite the distance, his arrow found its mark and Julian was disappointed that he could not carry off its skin.

He now entered an avenue of great trees, whose tops formed as it were a triumphal arch leading into a forest. A young roe deer sprang out of a thicket, a buck appeared within a clearing, a badger shuffled out of a hole and a peacock stood on the grass spreading its tail. No sooner had he slain them than more deer appeared, more bucks, more badgers, more peacocks, along with blackbirds, jays, polecats, foxes, hedgehogs and lynx. At every step forward Julian was confronted by an endless variety of beasts in ever greater numbers. They circled round him, trembling with fear and looking up at him with gentle pleading eyes. But Julian's thirst for slaughter was insatiable. Without pause or respite he fired his crossbow, drew his sword and stabbed with his knife, all extraneous thoughts, all memory of the past ousted from his mind. He lived only for the instant, a hunter in some unreal landscape, where time had lost all meaning and where everything occurred with that effortless ease which we experience in dreams. Suddenly his attention was caught by the most extraordinary sight. In front of him lay a small valley shaped like a circus arena and filled with wild deer. They stood huddled together in a group, warming each other with their breath, which hung like a cloud on the surrounding mist.

For a few moments, the prospect of such carnage as this left him breathless with pleasure. Then he dismounted, rolled up his sleeves and began shooting.

As the first of his arrows came whistling towards them, the stags all immediately turned their heads. Gaps suddenly began to appear in their midst, plaintive cries could be heard and a wave of panic ran through the whole group.

The lip of the valley was too high for the animals to cross; the hillsides enclosed them and they leapt about frantically, trying to find a way of escape. Julian continued to take aim and to fire; his arrows fell like driving rain in a thunderstorm. The stags, driven to a frenzy by this onslaught, ran at each other, rearing up on their hind legs and trying to climb up over each other. Their antlers became entangled and they fell together in a tumbling, writhing mound of bodies.

Eventually they died, stretched out on the sand, foaming at the mouth, their entrails spilling out on to the ground and the heaving of their bodies subsiding by degrees. Then all was still.

Night was drawing on and beyond the forest, through the gaps in the branches, the sky shone red like a lake of blood.

Julian leant against the trunk of a tree, gazing with amazement at the sheer scale of this carnage and unable to understand how he had managed to accomplish it.

Then, on the far side of the valley, at the forest's edge, he saw a stag and a hind with their fawn.

The stag was a huge black beast with massive antlers and a white beard. The hind was lighter in colour, the colour of faded leaves. She cropped the grass as she moved along, giving suck to her dappled fawn as she went.

Once more the sound of the crossbow broke the silence. The fawn was killed instantly. The mother raised her head to the skies and let out a deep, heart-rending, almost human cry of anguish. In sheer exasperation Julian shot an arrow full into her breast. The hind dropped to the ground.

The great stag had seen him and leapt forward. Julian fired his last arrow directly at him. It pierced his forehead and remained planted there.

But the stag did not seem to feel the arrow. It strode forward over the bodies of the hind and the fawn and came towards Julian, apparently bent on attacking him and tearing him to pieces. Julian backed away as it approached, speechless with terror. The huge beast stopped in front of him. A distant bell began to toll as, with eyes ablaze and in accents as solemn as a judge or a patriarch, the stag uttered this thrice-repeated warning:

'Beware! Beware! Beware! A curse lies upon you! One day, O savage heart, you will kill your father and your mother!'

The animal sank to its knees, closed its eyes and died.

Julian was astounded and then suddenly overcome with fatigue. A feeling of loathing and immense sadness welled up inside him. He placed his head in his hands and wept for a long time.

His horse was nowhere to be found and his dogs had deserted

him. The world seemed utterly desolate yet filled with vague
and threatening dangers. Julian, seized with panic, set off blindly
across country, took the first path he came to and found himself
almost at once back outside the castle gate.

That night he did not sleep. In the flickering light of the lamp
that hung above his bed, he kept seeing the great black stag. Its
warning preyed on his mind and he tried to convince himself it
could not be true. 'No, no, no!' he said to himself. 'I could not
possibly kill them!' But then he began to wonder, 'Yet what if I
should ever want to?' It terrified him to think that the Devil
might plant such a wish in his mind.

For three whole months his mother, in desperation, prayed at
his bedside while his father paced ceaselessly about the corridors
of the castle, bemoaning their misfortune. He summoned the
most famous physicians, who prescribed all manner of drugs.
Julian's illness, they said, was caused by some noxious wind or
amorous desire. But Julian simply shook his head to all the
questions they asked him.

Eventually his strength began to return and he was taken for
walks in the courtyard, with the old monk and the noble lord
each offering him an arm to lean on.

When he had completely recovered, he resolved that he would
never go hunting again.

In order to cheer him up, his father made him a present of a
great Saracen sword. The sword hung amongst a collection of
other trophies at the top of a stone pillar and they needed a
ladder to reach it. Julian climbed up the ladder but the sword
was too heavy for him and it slipped from his hand, falling so
close to the noble lord that it cut through his coat. Julian thought
he had killed his father and he fainted.

From that day on weapons filled him with dread. The mere
sight of a naked sword would make him turn pale. This weak-
ness was a cause of great disappointment to his family.

Eventually the old monk insisted in the name of God, family
honour and all his ancestors that Julian should once more take
up the pursuits that befitted his noble station.

Every day, to help pass the time, the squires would practise
throwing the javelin. Julian quickly became very adept at this.

He could land a javelin in the neck of a bottle, break the pointers on a weathervane or hit the studs on a door at a hundred paces.

One summer evening, just as the mist was beginning to make things indistinct, Julian was standing in the arbour in the castle garden when he noticed two white wings fluttering along the top of the wall at the far end of the alley. He was convinced it was a stork and he threw his javelin.

There was a piercing scream.

It was Julian's mother. Her bonnet with its two long flaps remained pinned to the wall.

Julian fled the castle and never came back.

2

He enlisted in a band of mercenaries that happened to be passing by.

He came to know hunger and thirst, fevers and vermin. He grew accustomed to the din of battle and the sight of death. The wind tanned his skin. His body became hardened by the wearing of armour and, as he was extremely strong, brave, temperate and intelligent, he was soon given command of a company.

When going into battle he would urge his soldiers forward with a great flourish of his sword. By means of a knotted rope he would scale the walls of citadels at night, buffeted by the gale, with flakes of Greek fire sticking to his cuirass and boiling resin and molten lead streaming down from the battlements. More than once his buckler was shattered by a stone dropped from above. Bridges overladen with men gave way beneath him. He once felled fourteen horsemen with his mace. He defeated all those who challenged him to single combat. On more than twenty occasions he was left for dead.

Through divine favour he always escaped alive, for he protected the clergy, orphans and widows and above all old men. Whenever he saw an old man walking in front of him he would call out to him to show his face, as if he were afraid of killing one of them by mistake.

Runaway slaves, rebellious peasants, disinherited bastards

and other such desperadoes flocked to his flag and he formed an army of his own.

His army grew. Julian became famous and was much sought after.

He gave assistance in turn to the Dauphin of France, the King of England, the Knights Templars of Jerusalem, the Surena of the Parthian army, the Negus of Abyssinia and the Emperor of Calicut. He fought against Scandinavians covered with fish-scales, Negroes with round shields made of hippopotamus skin and riding red donkeys, gold-skinned Indians brandishing broad sabres that flashed like mirrors above their diadems. He defeated the Troglodytes and the Anthropophagi. He travelled through lands that were so hot that the men's hair would catch fire like torches under the burning sun and others which were so cold that a soldier's arm might suddenly be severed from his body and fall to the ground. In some countries it was so foggy that they appeared to be marching forward surrounded by ghosts.

His advice was sought by a number of republics in times of difficulty. He negotiated with ambassadors and obtained terms that surpassed all expectation. If he heard that a king was behaving badly, he would suddenly present himself and remonstrate with him. He liberated nations that were oppressed. He rescued queens who were held captive in towers. It was none other than he who slew the Viper of Milan and the Dragon of Oberbirbach.

Now it so happened that the Emperor of Occitania, having defeated the Spanish Moors, had taken the sister of the Caliph of Cordoba as his concubine. As a result of this alliance he had acquired a daughter whom he had brought up as a Christian. The Caliph, however, pretending that he wished to be converted, came to visit him with a very sizeable escort, massacred his entire garrison, flung the Emperor into the deepest dungeon and proceeded to maltreat him in order to extort treasure from him.

Julian rushed to his aid, destroyed the army of infidels and killed the Caliph, cutting off his head and tossing it over the ramparts like a ball. He then released the Emperor from his prison and reinstalled him on his throne in the presence of his assembled court.

As a reward for these services, the Emperor offered Julian several basketloads of treasure, but he would not accept them. Thinking that Julian wanted to be paid more, the Emperor offered him three-quarters of all his wealth. Again Julian refused the offer. He then asked Julian to share his kingdom with him, but Julian politely declined. The Emperor was distraught; there seemed to be no way in which he could show his gratitude. Then suddenly he slapped his forehead and whispered something to one of his courtiers. Two tapestry curtains were drawn aside to reveal a young girl.

Her great dark eyes shone like two soft lights and her lips were parted in the most charming of smiles. The curls of her hair caught on the jewels of her dress, which she wore unbuttoned at the neck. The transparent gauze of her tunic revealed the outline of her young body. She was as pretty as a picture, with little dimples in her cheeks and a fine slender waist.

Julian was overcome with love, all the more so for having until then led a very chaste life.

So it was that Julian took the Emperor's daughter in marriage, along with a castle which she had inherited from her mother. Once the nuptials were completed and after endless protestations of mutual respect, the newly weds set off for their new home.

It was a palace of white marble in the Moorish style, situated on a promontory and surrounded by orange trees. A series of terraces planted out with flowers dropped down to the edge of a bay, where one could walk along the beach making the pink shells crackle underfoot. Behind the castle there was a forest, which spread out in the shape of a fan. The sky was forever blue and the trees swayed gently in the sea breeze or in the wind that blew from the mountains which bounded the distant horizon.

The rooms were carefully shaded from the full light of day and were lit by decorations inlaid into the walls. Tall columns, as slender as reeds, supported the domed ceilings, which were adorned with paintings in relief representing stalactites hanging from the roof of a grotto.

There were fountains in all the main rooms, mosaic tiling in the courtyards, carved panelling on the walls and countless other architectural refinements. The whole palace was so quiet that you could hear the rustle of a scarf or the echo of a sigh.

Julian no longer went to war. He now lived a life of leisure amongst a people at peace and every day a crowd of admirers came to do him homage, bending at the knee and kissing his fingers in the oriental fashion.

Dressed in purple, he would stand for hours at one of the bay windows, resting his elbows on the sill and dreaming of his hunting days, wishing he could ride out across the desert in search of ostrich and gazelle, lie in wait for leopards among the bamboo canes, track down rhinoceros in the forests, scale the most inaccessible mountain peaks in order to shoot at eagles or wrestle with polar bears on some ice-bound sea.

Sometimes, in a dream, he saw himself, like our forefather Adam in the Garden of Eden, surrounded by all the animals. By merely stretching out his arm he put them to death. Or else the animals filed past him two by two in order of size, from elephants and lions down to stoats and ducks, as on the day they went into Noah's ark. Julian lay hidden in the shadow of a cave and hurled javelins at them, never once missing his mark. There followed an unending succession of other animals; the slaughter went on and on; Julian would wake from his dream, his eyes rolling wildly.

Julian was often invited to go hunting by one or other of the many princes he had befriended. But he steadfastly refused their invitations, in the belief that this penance might avert his evil destiny, for he was convinced that his parents' fate was linked to the slaying of animals. It was a source of great sadness to him that he could not see his parents and his desire to do so was becoming unbearable.

His wife invited jugglers and dancers to the palace in order to entertain him.

She accompanied him on walks in the country, carried in an open litter. At other times they would lie together in a boat, peering over the edge at the fish as they darted about in water that was as clear as the light of day. Sometimes she would gather a handful of petals and throw them in his face. She would sit at his feet and play tunes on a three-stringed mandolin and then, placing her two hands on his shoulder, she would shyly ask: 'What ails you, dear husband?'

Sometimes he did not answer and sometimes he burst out sobbing. Then one day, he finally told her of his terrible fears.

She tried to reassure him, arguing, very reasonably, that his mother and father were in all probability already dead and that, should he ever see them again, there was nothing, whether it be by chance or design, that could possibly lead him to commit such a terrible crime. His fears were groundless and he ought to take up hunting again.

Julian smiled as he listened to her but he still could not be persuaded to yield to her advice.

One evening in August they were in their bedchamber. She had just got into bed and he was on his knees saying his prayers when he heard the bark of a fox followed by the scuffle of paws beneath the window. He could dimly make out the shapes of animals in the darkness. Temptation overcame him. He took his quiver from the wall.

His wife seemed surprised.

'I am doing as you bade me!' he said. 'I shall be back by sunrise.'

But she was afraid that something dreadful might happen to him.

He assured her that all would be well and left the room. Her changes of mood astonished him.

Shortly afterwards a page came to tell her that two strangers had arrived who, in the absence of his lordship, insisted on speaking with the lady of the castle immediately.

A few moments later, in came an old man and an old woman, bent at the back, covered in dust, dressed in coarse linen and each leaning on a stick.

Plucking up their courage, they announced that they had come to bring Julian news of his parents.

She leant forward to hear what they had to say.

They quickly exchanged glances and then asked whether Julian still loved his parents and whether he still spoke of them.

'Oh, yes,' she said.

'Well, we are they!' they cried and they sat down out of sheer weariness and exhaustion.

The young wife was far from convinced that her husband really was their son but they gave her proof by describing certain distinguishing marks on his body.

She leapt from her bed, called her page and had a meal brought to them.

Although they were both extremely hungry, they could eat hardly anything at all. Out of the corner of her eye she noticed that their bony hands shook as they lifted their goblets to their lips.

They plied her with endless questions about Julian. She answered them all but was careful to say nothing about Julian's fears concerning them.

When Julian had failed to return, they had left their castle in search of him. They had been wandering for several years, with only the vaguest hints of his whereabouts to guide them. But they had never given up hope of finding him. They had needed so much money to pay ferrymen and to stay at hostelries, to meet the dues of princes and the demands of robbers that their purse was now empty and they were reduced to beggary. But what did this matter, since very soon they would once again be able to hold their son in their arms! They extolled his good fortune in having such a charming wife; they could hardly take their eyes off her or refrain from kissing her.

They were amazed at the opulent furnishings of the room. The old man, having carefully examined the walls, asked why they bore the coat of arms of the Emperor of Occitania.

'The Emperor is my father,' she replied.

The old man gave a start, recalling the gypsy's prophecy, while the old woman remembered the words of the hermit. No doubt her son's success was but a prelude to the greater glories to come. They sat there open-mouthed in the light of the candelabrum that stood on the table.

They must have been a very handsome couple in their youth. The mother still had a fine head of hair, which fell in delicate tresses to the bottom of her cheeks like drifts of snow, while the father, with his tall build and his long beard, looked like a statue in a church.

Julian's wife urged them not to wait up for him. She installed them in her own bed and closed the casement window. Soon they were sound asleep. Day was just about to dawn and outside the window the birds were beginning to sing.

Meanwhile, Julian had slipped out of the palace gardens and was making his way through the forest. He walked with eager anticipation, enjoying the soft feel of the turf beneath his feet and the sweetness of the air.

The trees cast shadows over the mossy ground. Here and there patches of white moonlight showed in the clearings and he picked his way forward more cautiously, thinking that this might be a pool of water or the grass-green surface of a stagnant pond. There was not a sound to be heard. The animals, which a few minutes before had been prowling around his castle, were now nowhere to be seen.

The forest grew thicker and the darkness more intense. Wafts of warm air blew by him, laden with scents which dulled his senses. He found himself sinking into heaps of dead leaves and leant against an oak tree to catch his breath.

Suddenly, just behind him, a darker shape leapt across his path – a wild boar. Julian had no time to take up his bow and felt grieved by this as if by some terrible misfortune.

As he emerged from the wood he caught sight of a wolf running alongside a hedge.

Julian fired an arrow at it. The wolf stopped, turned its head to look at Julian and then continued on its way. It trotted on ahead of him, always keeping the same distance and occasionally stopping. But the minute Julian took aim with his bow it would start to run forward again.

The pursuit led Julian across an endless plain and over a succession of sandhills until finally he found himself on a high plateau which looked out over a vast stretch of country beyond. The ground was scattered with great flat stones which lay among the crumbling ruins of burial vaults. He stumbled over the bones of the dead; here and there worm-eaten crosses leant at pitiful angles. He saw vague shapes moving in the shadow of the tombs; suddenly out sprang a pack of startled hyenas, panting heavily. They came up to him, their claws tapping on the stones, and sniffed around him, baring their teeth to their gums. Julian drew his sword. The hyenas immediately scattered in all directions, scuttling off as fast as they could and disappearing in the distance in a cloud of dust.

An hour later he came across a wild bull in a ravine, its horns lowered and scraping the sand with its hoof. Julian thrust his lance into its neck. The lance shattered as if the animal had been made of bronze. Julian closed his eyes, thinking his end had come. When he opened them again, the bull had disappeared.

At this, Julian's soul was overcome with shame. He felt that his strength was being drained by some higher power. He decided to return home and turned back into the forest.

The forest had now become choked with creepers. He was beginning to clear a way through them with his sword when a marten suddenly slipped between his legs, a panther leapt over his shoulder and a snake wound its way up an ash tree.

In the leaves of the ash tree there was an enormous jackdaw looking down at him; suddenly he became aware of a great twinkling of lights, scattered among the branches, as though the heavens had rained down all their stars upon the forest. They were the eyes of animals – wild cats, squirrels, owls, parrots and monkeys.

Julian shot his arrows at them but the feathered shafts dropped gently on to the leaves of the tree like a flutter of white butterflies. He threw stones at them but the stones missed their mark and fell back to the ground. He cursed his luck. He felt utterly thwarted. He screamed and swore and choked with rage.

And then all the animals that he had been hunting reappeared, forming a tight circle around him. Some sat on their haunches, others stood on all fours. Julian stood in the middle of them, frozen with terror and unable to move a muscle. By a supreme effort of will, he managed to take one step forward. The birds that were perched up in the trees spread their wings, the creatures that stood on the ground stretched their limbs and the whole company set off with him.

The hyenas went in front of him; the wolf and the wild boar came behind. On his right walked the bull, swaying its head from side to side, and on his left the snake slithered through the grass, while the panther, arching its back, paced stealthily along beside. Julian walked as slowly as he could so as not to annoy them. Other animals appeared out of the bushes to swell the throng – porcupines, foxes, vipers, jackals and bears.

Julian began to run; the animals ran with him. The snake hissed; other animals slavered at the mouth and filled the air with their foul stench. The wild boar prodded his heels with its tusks and the wolf wiped its whiskery muzzle on the palms of his hands. The monkeys pinched him and pulled faces at him; the marten twisted itself around his feet. One of the bears knocked his hat off with a swipe of its paw and the panther, with a gesture of contempt, threw away one of Julian's arrows which it had been carrying in its mouth.

It was clear from the tricks that they played on him that the animals were making fun of Julian. They looked at him out of the corner of their eyes and seemed to be working out some plan of revenge. His ears were deafened by the buzz of insects, his face smarted from the whipping of birds' tails and he felt he was being suffocated by the breath of animals. He walked forward like a blind man, his arms outstretched and his eyes closed, without even the strength to cry for mercy.

A cock-crow rang in the air. Others followed. It was morning. Beyond the tops of the orange trees he recognized the roof of his palace.

Then, at the edge of a field, just three paces away from him, he saw a flock of red partridges fluttering among the stubble. He unfastened his cloak and threw it down over them like a net. But when he lifted the cloak up, there was only one partridge there. It had been dead for a long time and was already rotten.

This disappointment upset him more than all the others. His thirst for slaughter returned; since he could not kill animals he would gladly kill men.

He climbed the three terraces and thrust open the door with a blow of his fist. But at the foot of the staircase the thought of his dear wife softened his heart. She was no doubt asleep in bed. He would go up and give her a surprise.

He took off his sandals, turned the key gently in the lock and went in.

The leaded window panes darkened the early morning light. Julian caught his foot in some clothes on the floor and, walking forward, he bumped into a side table still laden with dishes. 'She must have had something to eat,' he thought and went towards the bed, which stood in a dark corner at the far end of the room. As he came to the bedside in order to kiss his wife, he leant over the pillow upon which the two heads reclined side by side. He felt the touch of a beard against his mouth.

He drew back with a start, thinking that he must be going mad. But he came back to the bed and ran his fingers over the covers until they came to rest on some very long strands of hair. Still convinced that he must be mistaken, he slowly passed his hand over the pillow a second time. This time there was no doubt about it; it was a beard. There was a man in his bed! A man sleeping with his wife!

In a rush of unbridled fury he leapt upon them, stabbing them repeatedly with his dagger. He smote the ground with his feet, foamed at the mouth and howled like a wild beast. At last he stood still. The two dead bodies lay in front of him, pierced through the heart; they had not even moved. He listened intently to the concerted rattle of their dying breath and as it subsided it was taken up by another sound from somewhere far away. He heard it only faintly at first – a plaintive voice, but persistent, and gradually coming nearer, getting louder and more cruel. With horror, Julian recognized the belling of the great black stag.

As he turned round, he saw framed in the doorway what he imagined was the ghost of his wife holding a lamp in her hand.

She had been drawn to the room by the noise of the murder. She took one look at the scene in front of her and realized immediately what had happened. She fled in horror, dropping the burning lamp on the floor.

Julian picked it up.

In front of him lay his mother and father, stretched on their backs with a hole in their hearts. There was a look of serene majesty on their faces, which spoke of some secret that they would now guard for eternity. There were splashes and smears of blood on their white bodies, the bedsheets and the floor and even on the ivory crucifix which hung in the alcove. The sunlight shining through the stained-glass window gave a bright crimson hue to the bloodstains and seemed to spread them in profusion to every part of the room. Julian approached the two dead bodies telling himself and willing himself to believe that this was not possible, that he must be mistaken, that people can sometimes look incredibly alike. At last he leant forward to look at the old man more closely; between the half-closed eyelids he saw the lifeless stare of a pupil that burnt into him like fire. He then went round to the other side of the bed where the second body lay, its face half hidden by its long white hair. He lifted the curls with his fingers and raised the head. He looked at it, one of his hands outstretched to support it, the other holding the lamp to give light. Drops of blood seeped out of the mattress and fell one by one on the floor.

At the end of the day, he appeared before his wife and in a voice altogether different from his own he told her firstly that she must never again speak to him, come near him or even look at him. In addition, under pain of damnation, she must obey all his orders, which were irrevocable.

The funeral rites were to be conducted according to the written instructions he had left on a prayer stool in the bedroom where his dead parents lay. He was leaving her his palace, his vassals and all he possessed. He would not even keep the clothes he stood up in or his sandals, which she would find at the top of the stairs.

In causing him to commit his crime she had simply obeyed the will of God. She must now pray for his soul since from this day forward he ceased to exist.

The dead were buried with great ceremony in a monastery chapel three days' journey from the castle. The funeral procession was followed at a distance by a hooded monk whom no one dared to speak to.

During the mass he remained prone in the centre of the doorway, his arms outstretched in the form of a cross and his face in the dust.

After the burial he was seen taking the road which led up into the mountains. Several times he turned to look back and finally disappeared from sight.

3

Julian went away never to return, begging for his daily bread in every corner of the world.

He would hold out his hand to horse riders as they approached him on the highroad, accost harvesters in the fields on bended knee or stand motionless at courtyard gates, and the expression on his face was always so sad that no one ever refused to give him alms.

He would further humble himself by telling his story, whereupon everyone fled his presence with copious signs of the cross. In villages he had already been to, as soon as people saw him coming they shut their doors, shouted threats and threw stones at him. The more charitably disposed would leave a bowl of food on their window sills and close the shutters to avoid seeing him.

Because he was everywhere rejected he avoided the company of men. He fed himself on roots, plants, wild fruits and shellfish which he gathered on the seashore.

Sometimes as he rounded a bend on a hillside he would see below him a jumble of tightly packed rooftops, with stone spires, bridges, towers and a tangle of dark streets whose steady buzz of activity floated up to where he stood.

His longing to share in the lives of others sometimes prompted him to walk down into the town. But the ugly expressions on people's faces, the noise they made as they went about their work and the triviality of their conversation brought a chill to his heart. On feast days when the great cathedral bell rang out from early morning, summoning all the townspeople to their merrymaking, he would see them leave their homes and stand watching the dances in the squares, the beer fountains at street corners and the damask awnings which adorned the town houses of the nobility. In the evening he would peer in at the ground-floor windows and see families gathered together at the dinner table with grandparents holding young children on their knees. Sobs choked him; he would turn away and retrace his footsteps out into the open country.

His heart leapt with joy whenever he saw a foal in a meadow, a bird in its nest or an insect settling on a flower. But if he tried to come near, it would either run off, hide itself in sheer terror or fly quickly away.

He sought out lonely places. But the moaning of the wind sounded to his ears like gasps of dying breath; the drops of dew as they fell to the ground reminded him of certain other drops which had fallen more heavily to the floor. Every evening the sun cast streaks of blood across the clouds and every night in his dreams the killing of his parents would begin afresh.

He made himself a hair shirt with iron spikes. Whenever he saw a chapel on top of a hill, he would climb up to it on his knees. But the unrelenting thought of his crime cast a shadow over the beauty of these sanctuaries and caused him even greater torture than the discomforts of his penance.

He did not rebel against God for having made him commit this act and yet the thought that he had actually perpetrated it filled him with despair.

He felt such loathing for his own body that in the hope of gaining release from it he subjected himself to the worst sorts of danger. He rescued the halt and lame from fires and children from bottomless chasms. But he rose from the abyss and walked unscathed from the flames.

Time did not ease his suffering. It became more than he could bear and he resolved to die.

One day he was standing beside a pool and as he leant over it to gauge the depth of the water he saw the face of an old man appear in front of him, thin and gaunt, wearing a white beard and looking so pitiful that he could not restrain his tears. As Julian wept, so too did the face. Julian did not recognize his own reflection and vaguely remembered having seen a face like this before. He let out a cry. It was his father! All thought of killing himself vanished.

And so Julian roamed from country to country, bearing the burden of his terrible memories. Eventually he came to a river which was dangerous to cross because of the swift current and because there was a broad stretch of mud along its banks. No one had dared to cross it for a very long time.

An old boat lay amongst the reeds, its stern buried in the mud and its bows pointing upwards. Julian examined it and discovered a pair of oars and it occurred to him that here was a way of placing his life at the service of others.

He began by building a makeshift causeway on the river-bank which would allow people to reach the water. He tore his fingernails trying to lift out the huge boulders, he hoisted them on to his chest to carry them, slipped and sank into the mud and on several occasions he nearly lost his life.

Next he repaired the boat with bits of wreckage and built himself a little hut out of tree-trunks and clay.

Once the ferry was known about, travellers came to use it. They hailed him from the opposite bank of the river by waving flags and Julian would straight away jump into his boat. The boat was very heavy and was further weighed down with all manner of bags and bundles, not to mention the packhorses who were frightened of the water and difficult to keep under control, which further added to the confusion. Julian asked for nothing in return for his troubles, although some gave him leftover scraps of food from their bags or worn-out clothes that they had no further use for. Some of the more unruly passengers would shout and swear. Julian would gently rebuke them, only to be sworn at himself. His answer to this was simply to give them his blessing.

A little table, a stool, a bed of dried leaves and three earthenware drinking cups were all the furniture he possessed. Two holes in the wall served as windows. On one side, as far as the eye could see, stretched a vast empty plain, scattered with pale patches of standing water, and in front of him flowed the dull green waters of the great river. In spring the damp earth gave out a smell of decay. Then would come a fierce wind, raising swirling clouds of dust that settled everywhere, tainting the drinking water and filling Julian's mouth with grit. A little later there were swarms of mosquitoes that buzzed in his ears and stung him incessantly day and night. Finally he had to endure dreadful frosts which made everything as hard as stone and filled him with an insane desire to devour meat.

Months would go by without Julian seeing a living soul. Often he would close his eyes, trying to remember the past and return to the days of his youth. In his mind's eye he would see the courtyard of a castle with greyhounds on the front steps, page-boys in the armoury and a young boy with blond hair standing beneath an arbour of climbing vines between an old man dressed in furs and a woman wearing a tall coif. And then suddenly he would see two corpses. He would throw himself flat on his bed, weeping and crying over and over again:

'Ah! My poor father! My poor mother! My poor mother!' He would eventually fall into an uneasy sleep in which these gloomy visions continued to haunt him.

One night as he lay asleep he thought he heard someone calling him. He strained his ears but all he could hear was the rushing of the water.

Then he heard the voice again:

'Julian!'

It was coming from the other side of the river, which seemed extraordinary as the river was very broad at this point.

The voice called a third time:

'Julian!'

It was a high-pitched voice and sounded like the pealing of a church bell.

Julian lit his lantern and went out of his hut. Out in the night a violent storm was raging. It was pitch-black with only the white crests of the waves to relieve the darkness.

After a moment's hesitation, Julian cast off from the shore. Immediately the water became calm. The boat slipped easily through it and reached the other bank where a man stood waiting for him.

He was wrapped in a tattered linen cloth, his face resembled a plaster mask and his eyes were redder than blazing coals. Julian held the lantern up to look at him and saw that his body was covered with the most hideous sores of leprosy. And yet there was in his bearing something majestic and regal.

As soon as he stepped into the boat it sank down heavily in the water beneath his weight. It righted itself again with a surge and Julian began to row.

With every pull of the oars the waves flung the prow of the boat in the air. The water was as black as ink and rushed past furiously on both sides of the boat. The waves formed deep troughs and then rose up like mountain walls; the boat leapt upwards over the crests and plummeted back down into the depths, where it spun round, tossed about by the wind.

Julian bent himself forward, stretched out his arms and arched himself backwards with his feet so that he could row more strongly. Hailstones stung his hands, rain ran down his back, the force of the wind took his breath away and he could row no more. The boat was swept downstream by the current. But Julian knew that this was no ordinary undertaking, that this was a command he could not fail to obey. Once more he took to his task and the rattle of the rowlocks sounded clear above the din of the storm.

The little lantern shone in front of him, its light occasionally hidden by birds as they flew past it. But all the time he could see the eyes of the leper shining steadily from where he stood in the stern of the boat, as still as a column of stone.

This continued for a long time, for a very long time.

When they reached the hut, Julian closed the door and saw the leper seated on the stool. The shroud-like cloth which he had been wrapped in had fallen to his waist to reveal his shoulders, chest and scrawny arms, completely covered in scabs and sores. Deep furrows scored his brow. Like a skeleton, he had a hole where his nose should have been. His lips were blue and from his mouth came waves of foul-smelling breath as thick as fog.

'I am hungry,' he said.

Julian gave him what he had – an old piece of bacon and the

crusts from a loaf of black bread. After he had finished eating, the table, the stool and the handle of the knife bore the same marks that could be seen on his body.

Then he said: 'I am thirsty.'

Julian went to get his jug. As he picked it up it released a fragrance that warmed his heart and made his nostrils dilate. It was wine. What good fortune! But the leper stretched out his hand and drank the whole jug at one draught.

Then he said: 'I am cold.'

Julian took his candle and lit a bundle of bracken in the middle of the hut.

The leper drew forward to warm himself at the fire. He crouched on his heels and began to tremble all over. Julian could see that he was growing weaker. The light had gone from his eyes, his sores were oozing. Suddenly in a voice that was barely a whisper he murmured: 'Your bed!'

Julian gently helped him to drag himself on to the bed and even spread the sail of his boat over him as a bed-cover.

The leper lay there moaning. The corners of his lips parted to reveal his teeth, his chest heaved as his dying breaths became quicker and quicker and with each breath he took his stomach sank down to his backbone.

Then his eyes closed.

'My bones are like ice,' he said. 'Come and lie beside me.'

Julian lifted the sail and lay down on the dried leaves beside him.

The leper turned his head towards him.

'Take off your clothes so that I may feel the warmth of your body.'

Julian took off his clothes. Then, naked as on the day he was born, he got back into the bed. Against his thigh he could feel the leper's skin, as cold as a snake and as rough as a file.

Julian whispered words of comfort but the leper could only stammer in reply: 'Ah, I am going to die. Come closer. Give me your warmth. No, not just with your hands. Give me your whole body.'

Julian lay down at full length on top of the leper, mouth to mouth, breast to breast.

The leper clasped him in his arms. And all at once his eyes shone with starry splendour, his hair spread out like rays of sunshine and the breath from his nostrils smelt as sweet as roses. A cloud of incense rose from the hearth and the waves outside began to sing. In the same instant Julian felt as it were a flood of boundless delights and unearthly bliss entering his enraptured soul. And he in whose arms he lay grew taller and taller until his head and feet touched the two walls of the hut. The roof flew off and the firmament opened above them. Julian rose up into the blue, into the open arms of Our Lord Jesus Christ, who bore him up to Heaven.

And that is the story of Saint Julian Hospitator almost exactly as you will find it told in a stained-glass window in a church near to where I was born.[5]

HERODIAS

I

The citadel of Machaerus[1] stood to the east of the Dead Sea on an outcrop of basalt shaped like a cone. It was surrounded by four deep valleys, one on each side, one in front and one behind. Around the base of the rock was a cluster of houses, enclosed within a circular wall that rose and fell as it followed the contours of the land on which it was built. A zigzag road hewn out of the rock connected the town below with the fortress, whose walls were a hundred and twenty cubits high and built at irregular angles with battlements along the edges and towers dotted along them that looked rather like the ornamental points on this crown of stone, perched high above the abyss.

Inside there was a palace graced with colonnades and a terrace-roof enclosed by a sycamore balustrade and a series of tall poles which were designed to carry an awning.

One morning just before daybreak, the Tetrarch Herod Antipas came to lean on the balustrade and looked out over the surrounding country.

The mountain peaks immediately beneath him were just beginning to show themselves, although the lower slopes and the valley floors were still shrouded in darkness.

The lingering morning mists parted to reveal the outline of the Dead Sea. The sun rose behind Machaerus, spreading a red glow across the landscape and gradually lighting up the sandy sea shore, the hills and the desert and, away in the distance, the rugged grey contours of the mountains of Judaea. In the middle distance, Engedi appeared as a long black line, while further off was the round dome of Mount Hebron. He could see Eshcol with its pomegranates, Sorek with its vines, Karmel with its fields of sesame and the huge square Tower of Antonia rising above the city of Jerusalem. The Tetrarch turned away and looked at the palm trees of Jericho on his right and thought of all the other towns in his Galilee – Capernaum, Endor, Nazareth and Tiberias – that he would perhaps never see again. The river Jordan flowed across the arid plain, which stretched out beneath him, glistening white like a carpet of snow. At this time of day the lake looked as though it were made of lapis lazuli. At its southernmost tip, towards the Yemen, Antipas saw what he feared he might see – an encampment of brown tents, men carrying spears and moving about among their horses, the dying embers of campfires shining like sparks on the ground.

This was the army of the King of the Arabs, whose daughter he had renounced in order to marry Herodias, the wife of one of his brothers, who, because he had no pretensions to power, had gone to live in Italy.

Antipas was waiting for assistance from the Romans. But Vitellius, the Governor of Syria, had not arrived and Antipas was becoming extremely anxious.

Perhaps Agrippa had spoken ill of him to the Emperor.[2] His third brother, Philip, the ruler of Batanea, was secretly taking up arms. The Jews had had enough of his idolatry and everyone else had had enough of the way he ruled. He was now faced with two possible courses of action: either he could try to conciliate the Arabs, or he could conclude an alliance with the Parthians. On the pretext of celebrating his birthday, he had chosen this day to invite the leaders of his army, the governors of the local regions and all the chief men of Galilee to a great banquet.

He carefully scanned the roads leading to the citadel. They were deserted. A group of eagles hovered above him; the soldiers along the ramparts had fallen asleep leaning against the walls. Nothing stirred inside the castle.

Suddenly he heard a distant voice that seemed to come from the very depths of the earth. His face turned pale. He leant forward to listen but the voice had stopped. Then he heard it again. Antipas clapped his hands and called out: 'Mannaeï! Mannaeï!'

A man appeared, naked to the waist like a masseur at a public bathhouse. He was old and thin and very tall and at his side he carried a cutlass in a bronze scabbard. His hair was held back with a comb, which emphasized the height of his forehead. His eyes were dulled with sleep but his teeth shone white and he walked lightly over the flagstones on the tips of his toes, his whole body as lithe as a monkey's and his face as expressionless as a mummy's.

'Where is he?' asked the Tetrarch.

Mannaeï pointed to something behind them with his thumb. 'Still in there,' he said.

'I thought I heard him.'

Antipas gave a great sigh of relief and began to ask about Jokanaan, the man whom the Romans called John the Baptist. Had anyone spoken to the two men who had been allowed to visit him in his cell the other month? Had anyone discovered what had brought them here?

'There was an exchange of cryptic words,' Mannaeï replied, 'like thieves meeting each other at night at some crossroads. Then they went off towards Upper Galilee, saying that they would return bearing wondrous news.'

Antipas lowered his head and a look of fear crossed his face.

'Guard him! Guard him well!' he said. 'Let no one in to see him! Make sure the door is locked! Cover the pit! No one must even know he is alive!'

Mannaeï did not need to be told; the orders had already been carried out, for Jokanaan was a Jew and, like all Samaritans, Mannaeï detested Jews.

Their own temple at Gerizim, which Moses had decided should be the centre of Israel, had been destroyed during the reign of King Hyrcanus.[3] The Temple at Jerusalem infuriated them; they saw it as an affront, a permanent injustice. Mannaeï was among those who had broken into it to desecrate the altar with human remains. His companions, who had not managed to make their getaway as quickly as he, had all been beheaded.

He could see it now in the gap between the two hills with the sun glinting on its white marble walls and the gold lining of its roof. It looked like an iridescent mountain, something superhuman, reducing everything around it to nothing by its arrogant display of opulence.

Mannaeï stretched out his arms towards Zion. Drawing himself up to his full height and clenching his fists, he hurled a curse at it, convinced that the words alone had the power to bring about his wish.

Antipas listened to him without appearing the slightest bit shocked.

The Samaritan continued:

'At times he becomes agitated, wants to escape and hopes he will be rescued. At other times he lies there quietly like a sick animal. Sometimes I have seen him pacing about in the dark saying over and over again: "What does it matter? If his reign is to come, mine must end!" '[4]

Antipas and Mannaeï looked at each other. But the Tetrarch was in no mood to think about these things.

The mountains all around him, heaped on top of each other like great waves of stone, the dark clefts in the cliff walls, the vast expanse of blue sky, the blinding light of the sun and the yawning chasms beneath him disturbed his mind. His spirits sank as he looked out over the desert; in its folds and convolutions he seemed to see the shapes of ruined amphitheatres and palaces. The warm wind brought a smell of sulphur, as if exuded by the two godforsaken cities that now lay buried beneath the shores of that leaden sea. These signs of divine wrath struck terror into his heart. He stood there with his elbows on the balustrade, his head in his hands, staring in front of him. He felt the touch of a hand and turned round. Herodias stood before him.

She was dressed in a light purple gown that reached down to her sandals. She had left her room in a hurry and was wearing neither necklaces nor earrings. A tress of her dark hair fell down on to her arm and disappeared between her breasts. Her nostrils were dilated and quivering. There was a look of joy and triumph on her face. She shook the Tetrarch and shouted:

'Caesar is our friend! Agrippa is in prison!'

'Who told you?' he said.

'I just know it!'

'It is because he wanted Caius to be Emperor!'[5] she added.

All the time Agrippa had been living under their protection he had solicited the title of king, which they had coveted just as much as he. They now no longer had anything to fear.

'Tiberius does not usually let his prisoners go free and life inside one of his dungeons is sometimes anything but assured,' said Herodias.

Antipas understood what she meant and, even though she was Agrippa's own sister, her murderous intent seemed to him perfectly justified. Such killings were part of the natural order of things, an inevitable consequence of belonging to a royal household. In Herod's, they had lost count of them.

Then Herodias explained how she had plotted Agrippa's downfall; how she had bribed his colleagues, opened his letters and posted spies at every door, how she had seduced Eutychus who then betrayed him to Caesar.

'It was a small price to pay!' she said. 'Have I not done more for you already? Have I not abandoned my own daughter?'

After her divorce, she had left her daughter in Rome, hoping to have other children by the Tetrarch. She never spoke of her and Antipas wondered what had prompted this sudden display of affection.

The awning had been opened out and some large cushions were hurriedly placed beside them. Herodias sank down on to them and, turning her back to the Tetrarch, began to weep. Presently she wiped her eyes with her hand and said that she did not want to think about it any more and that she was happy. She reminded him of their conversations together in the atrium back in Rome, their meetings at the baths, their walks along the Via Sacra, the evenings spent in splendid villas, sitting beneath arches of flowers, listening to the murmur of fountains and looking out over the Roman Campagna. She looked at him as she used to do then, pressing her body gently against his breast and caressing him with her hands. He pushed her away. The love that she was trying to rekindle was now a thing of the past. It was also the cause of all his misfortunes; the war had been going on now for nearly twelve years and it had aged the Tetrarch. Beneath his dark, violet-edged toga his shoulders were

bent with care; his long white hair mingled with his beard and
the sunlight, as it filtered through the awning, lit up the wrinkles
on his brow. There were wrinkles on Herodias' brow too. They
sat there face to face, looking at each other angrily.

The mountain roads were beginning to fill with people –
herdsmen driving cattle, children pulling donkeys and stablemen
leading their horses. Those coming down from the hills beyond
Machaerus disappeared from view behind the castle but others
were coming up the ravine in front of them and could be seen
arriving at the town and unloading their bags in the courtyards.
These were servants arriving ahead of the Tetrarch's guests as
well as his own men bringing provisions.

Suddenly at the far end of the terrace, to their left, they saw
an Essene coming towards them,[6] barefoot, dressed in a white
robe, a man of strikingly ascetic appearance. Mannaeï rushed
forward from the right, brandishing his sword.

'Kill him!' Herodias shouted.

'Stop!' cried the Tetrarch.

Mannaeï came to a halt and stood motionless. The Essene did
likewise.

Then they both withdrew, walking backwards without taking
their eyes off each other and disappearing down two separate
staircases.

'I know that man!' said Herodias. 'His name is Phanuel and
he is trying to see Jokanaan. Keeping him alive is just madness!'

Antipas insisted that some day he might be of use. His attacks
on Jerusalem were winning the other Jews over to them.

'No!' she replied. 'The Jews will accept any ruler they are
given. They are simply incapable of forming a country of their
own!' The most sensible thing to do with someone who raised
their hopes about prophecies made in the time of Nehemiah[7]
was to get rid of him.

The Tetrarch's view was that there was no hurry. And as for
Jokanaan being a danger to them, nothing could be further from
the truth. He pretended to laugh.

'Be quiet!' said Herodias. And once again she told him how
she had been humiliated when on her way to the balsam harvest
in Gilead.

'I saw people on the river-bank putting their clothes back on. There was a man standing on a little mound near them, declaiming something. All he wore was a camel skin around his loins and his hair stood out like a lion's mane. As soon as he saw me he spat out a stream of curses from the prophets. His eyes were ablaze, he ranted and raved and raised his hands aloft as if trying to call down thunder from the skies. It was impossible to get away. The wheels of my chariot were up to their axles in the sand. I could only move forward very slowly, covering myself with my cloak and with my blood running cold at the deluge of insults that rained down upon me.'

Jokanaan was making life unbearable for her. The soldiers who had seized and bound him had been given instructions to stab him if he tried to resist. But he had given himself up without a struggle. They had put snakes in his prison: the snakes had all died.

Herodias was furious that these ploys had failed. She still could not understand what he had against her or what he stood to gain. He had proclaimed his ideas to huge crowds of people; they had spread far and wide and were still circulating. Wherever she went she heard people talking of them; they filled the air. If she had had to defend herself against an army of legionaries she would have had the courage to do so, but this was a power more insidious than the sword, something intangible and quite extraordinary. She paced about the terrace, white with anger and unable to find words to express her frustration.

It had also occurred to her that the Tetrarch might give in to public opinion and decide to renounce her. If that happened, all would be lost. Ever since childhood she had dreamed of ruling over a great empire. This is what had prompted her to leave her first husband and marry this one, who she now thought had been deceiving her.

'Much good it did me, marrying into your family!' she said.

'My family is as good as yours,' said the Tetrarch blandly.

Herodias felt the blood of her ancestors, that noble line of kings and priests, boiling in her veins.

'But your grandfather was a floor-sweeper in the temple at Askalon and the rest of your family were just shepherds, robbers or muleteers, a rabble, and in thrall to Judah since the time of King David! My ancestors have all beaten yours in battle! You were chased out of Hebron by the first of the Maccabees and forced to accept circumcision by Hyrcanus!' Her voice shook with the contempt that the patrician bears the plebeian, the hatred of Jacob for Esau. She accused him of being indifferent to insults, too tolerant towards the Pharisees who were betraying him and a coward in the face of his own people who detested her. 'You detest me as much as they do, admit it! You would rather be back with that Arab girl who used to dance round the stones. Well, take her back! Go and live with her under her canvas roof! Eat the bread she bakes in the ashes! Drink her sour ewe's milk! Kiss her blue cheeks! Forget you ever knew me!'

The Tetrarch was no longer listening to her. He was looking down at the flat roof of a house on which he could see a young girl and an old woman. The woman was holding a parasol with a reed handle as long as a fishing rod. In the middle of the carpet a large travelling basket lay open, full to the brim with waistbands, veils and jewelled pendants. From time to time the girl would lean forward and brandish something from the contents of the basket in the air. She was dressed, as was usual for Roman girls, in a pleated tunic and a peplum with emerald tassels. Her hair was held back by blue ribbons and from time to time she put her hand up to it as if it were too heavy for her. The shadow from the parasol fell across her, half hiding her from view. Now and then Antipas caught brief glimpses of her delicate neck, the corner of an eye, the shape of a little mouth. But he could see the whole of her upper body from her hips to her neck, so lissom and supple as she leant forward and then straightened herself again. He waited for her to repeat the movement; his breathing quickened and his eyes lit up. Herodias stood watching him.

'Who is that?' he asked.

Herodias replied that she had no idea and walked away, her anger suddenly calmed.

A number of people were waiting under the colonnade to see the Tetrarch. There were some Galileans, the chief scribe, the steward of the pasture-lands, the chief administrator of the salt mines and a Babylonian Jew who was in charge of his cavalry. They all greeted him together. Antipas then disappeared towards the inner rooms.

Phanuel appeared round the corner of a corridor.

'Ah, you again!' said the Tetrarch. 'I suppose you have come to see Jokanaan.'

'And to see you too! I have something very important to tell you.'

He walked along behind him and followed him into a dimly lit room.

A little daylight found its way through a grill which ran the length of the wall just below the cornice. The walls were painted garnet-red, almost black. At the far end of the room there was a bed made of ebony with oxhide webbing. Above it hung a golden shield which gleamed like a sun.

Antipas walked across the room and lay down on the bed.

Phanuel remained standing. He raised his arm and, speaking as one inspired, said:

'From time to time the Almighty sends us one of His sons. Jokanaan is one of them. If you maltreat him you will be punished.'

'It is he who is persecuting me,' exclaimed Antipas. 'He asked me to do something which was impossible and ever since then he has made my life a misery. I was not hard on him to begin with. But he has sent men out from Machaerus who are spreading chaos throughout my provinces! Woe betide him! If he chooses to attack me, I must defend myself!'

'Yes, his anger is too violent,' said Phanuel. 'But no matter, you must release him.'

'One does not release wild beasts,' said the Tetrarch.

'Have no fear,' replied the Essene. 'He will go amongst the Arabs, the Gauls and the Scythians. He must take his message to the ends of the earth!'

Antipas seemed lost in a dream.

'He possesses great power! . . . I cannot help liking him!'

'Then why not let him go free!'

The Tetrarch shook his head. He feared Herodias and Mannaeï. He feared the unknown.

Phanuel tried to make him change his mind, promising that
the Essenes would swear allegiance to the kings. His plans would
be sure of success, for everyone respected these poor men who
defied torture, went about dressed in flax and read the future in
the stars.

Antipas remembered something Phanuel had said a moment
or so earlier.

'You said there was something important you had to tell me.'

Just then a Negro rushed into the room, his body white with
dust. He was gasping for breath and all he could say was:

'Vitellius!'[8]

'What? Is he coming?'

'I have seen him. He will be here within three hours!'

The curtains in the corridors were shaken as if by the wind.
The castle was filled with noise – the sounds of running feet,
furniture being dragged about, silverware clattering to the floor.
From the tops of the towers trumpets were being sounded to
alert the slaves all over the castle.

2

A great crowd of people had gathered on the ramparts when
Vitellius entered the courtyard. He was leaning on the arm of
his interpreter and behind him there followed a huge red litter
adorned with plumes and mirrors. He wore the toga, the laticlave[9] and the laced boots of a consul and was surrounded by
lictors.

The lictors walked up to the castle gate and set down their
twelve fasces, bundles of rods bound together by a strap with
an axe in the middle. At this, everyone trembled before the
majesty of the Roman people.

The litter, which was being carried by eight men, came to a
stop. Out of it stepped a youth with a fat paunch, a face covered
in spots and strings of pearls on his fingers. He was offered a
large cup of spiced wine. He drank it and asked for another.

The Tetrarch was grovelling at the knees of the Proconsul,
explaining how upset he was that he had not learnt earlier that
he was to be honoured with his presence. Had he known, he

would have made proper arrangements to receive him along
the way. The Vitellii were descended from the goddess Vitellia.
The road that led from the Janiculum to the sea still bore their
name. Their family could boast countless quaestorships and
consulships and as for Lucius, who was now his guest, they
owed him a debt of gratitude as conqueror of the Clites and
father of the young Aulus, who might be said to be coming back
to his homeland, since the East was the home of the gods. These
effusive compliments were spoken in Latin. Vitellius listened to
them impassively.

He replied by saying that no one could have brought greater
glory to a nation than great King Herod.[10] The Athenians had
entrusted him with the supervision of the Olympic games. He
had built temples in honour of Augustus. He had been patient,
ingenious and redoutable and he had always remained loyal to
the Caesars.

Between the columns with their bronze capitals they saw
Herodias coming towards them. She moved forward like an
empress, surrounded by women and eunuchs who carried burning incense on silver-gilt platters.

The Proconsul took three steps towards her and bowed his
head in greeting.

'What a blessing it is', she exclaimed, 'that Agrippa, the enemy
of Tiberius, can now no longer harm us!'

Vitellius did not know what had happened but he sensed that
Herodias was a dangerous woman. When Antipas began to
insist that there was nothing he would not do for the Emperor,
Vitellius interrupted him and said:

'Even if you go behind someone else's back?'[11]

Vitellius had obtained hostages from the King of the Parthians
but the Emperor had not realized this because Antipas, who had
also been present at the negotiations, had sent the news off first
in order to get himself noticed. This was why Vitellius disliked
him so intensely and why he had been so slow in sending him
assistance.

The Tetrarch muttered an excuse, but Aulus laughed and
said:

'Calm down. I will look after you!'

The Proconsul pretended not to hear this. The father's prospects depended upon his son's depravity. This flower from the gutters of Capri[12] brought him so many advantages that he nurtured it carefully whilst at the same time treating it with caution because he knew it was poisonous.

There was a sudden commotion just outside the gate. A string of white mules was being led into the courtyard, ridden by men in priests' clothing. These were Sadducees and Pharisees who had all come to Machaerus with the same purpose in mind; the Sadducees wanted the office of High Priest to be conferred on them, whilst the Pharisees wanted to retain it for themselves. Their faces looked very serious, especially those of the Pharisees, who were hostile to Rome and the Tetrarch. The large borders of their tunics made it difficult for them to move among the crowd. Their tiaras were poised precariously on their foreheads above strips of vellum which had handwriting on them.

At almost the same moment a group of soldiers from the advance guard arrived. They had put their shields inside sacks to protect them from the dust. Behind them came Marcellus, the Proconsul's lieutenant, accompanied by some publicans[13] carrying wooden tablets held tightly under their arms.

Antipas introduced the principal members of his entourage: Tolmaï, Kanthera, Sehon, Ammonius of Alexandria who bought asphalt for him, Naaman the captain of his velites[14] and Jacim the Babylonian.

Vitellius had noticed Mannaeï.

'Who is that man over there?'

The Tetrarch explained with a gesture of his hand that he was the executioner.

Then he presented the Sadducees.

Jonathas, a short, loose-limbed man who spoke Greek, begged the master to honour them with a visit to Jerusalem. Vitellius said that he would probably be going there.

Eleazar, a man with a hooked nose and a long beard, appealed on behalf of the Pharisees for the return of the High Priest's cloak which the civil authorities held under lock and key in the Tower of Antonia.

Then the Galileans launched into a tirade against Pontius Pilate. Because some madman had gone hunting for King David's golden vases in a cave near Samaria, he had had some of the inhabitants killed. They all began speaking at once, Mannaeï more vociferously than the others. Vitellius promised them that the criminals would be punished.

There was a sudden clamour of angry voices opposite one of the colonnades, where the soldiers had hung their shields. The coverings had been removed and Caesar's effigy could be seen on the bosses. To the Jews this was a form of idolatry. Antipas went to remonstrate with them while Vitellius sat on a raised seat in the colonnade marvelling at their fury. Tiberius had done right to banish four hundred of them to Sardinia. But here in their own country their views could not be ignored and he ordered the shields to be removed.

Then they all crowded round the Proconsul begging him to remedy injustices and grant them privileges and alms. Clothes were being torn in the crush and slaves were hitting out right and left with sticks to clear some space. Those nearest the gate made their way out on to the road, only to meet others coming up in the other direction and to be driven back – two streams crossing each other in this jostling crowd of men, shut in by the surrounding walls.

Vitellius asked why there were so many people there. Antipas told him that it was because of the celebrations for his birthday and he pointed to his men leaning over the battlements and hoisting up huge baskets of meat, fruit, vegetables, antelopes and storks, great blue fish, grapes, watermelons and pomegranates piled up like pyramids. Aulus could not contain himself.[15] He rushed off in the direction of the kitchens, impelled by the gluttony that was later to astonish the whole world.

As he went past one of the wine cellars he caught sight of some large cooking-pots that looked like breastplates. Vitellius came over to look at them and asked to be shown the underground chambers of the fortress.

These were hewn out of the rock with high vaulted ceilings supported here and there by pillars. The first contained a collection of old armour but the second was filled with pikes, their

points protruding from bunches of feathers. The third looked
as though it were lined with reed mats, being filled with thin
arrows all stacked tightly together on their ends. The walls of
the fourth chamber were covered with scimitar blades. In the
middle of the fifth were rows of helmets, their curved crests
making them look like an army of red snakes. The sixth chamber
housed quivers, the seventh greaves and the eighth armlets. In
the remaining chambers there were forks, grappling hooks,
ladders, ropes and even poles for the catapults and bells for the
dromedaries' breastplates. Because the mountain grew broader
at its base, hollowed out inside like a beehive, beneath these
chambers there were a great many more, and even deeper than
the ones above.

Vitellius, Phineas his interpreter and Sisenna the chief publican inspected all of them by the light of torches carried by three
eunuchs.

In the darkness they made out some even grimmer objects
devised by the barbarians: bludgeons studded with nails,
poisoned javelins and iron pincers that looked like the jaws of
a crocodile. In short, in Machaerus the Tetrarch had sufficient
instruments of war for an army of forty thousand men.

He had gathered them together in case his enemies formed an
alliance against him. However, the Proconsul might very easily
imagine or assume that they were for fighting the Romans and
so he tried to think of ways of justifying himself.

Perhaps he should say that these arms were not his, that many
of them were used for defending themselves against marauders,
that they were needed as protection against the Arabs or that
they had all belonged to his father. And instead of walking
behind the Proconsul he walked on quickly ahead. At one point
he placed himself against the wall, spreading his arms and trying
to hide it with his toga. But the top of a door could be seen
above his head. Vitellius noticed it and wanted to know what
was inside.

He was told that the only person who could open it was the
Babylonian.

'Then call the Babylonian!' he ordered.

They waited for him to appear.

His father had come to Palestine from the banks of the Euphrates, offering his services to Herod the Great, along with five hundred horsemen, in defence of the eastern frontiers. When the kingdom was divided, Jacim had stayed with Philip and was now in the service of Antipas.

He arrived with a bow across his shoulders and carrying a whip. His bandy legs were bound round tightly with cords of different colours. He wore a sleeveless tunic which revealed his brawny arms and a fur cap which shaded his face. His beard was curled in ringlets.

At first he did not seem to understand the interpreter. Vitellius gave Antipas a quick glance and he promptly repeated the Proconsul's order. Jacim placed his hands on the door and it slid into the wall.

A gust of warm air blew out of the darkness. In front of them a winding passage led downwards. They followed it until they came to the mouth of a cavern, much larger than the other underground chambers.

At the far end was an arched opening in the wall giving out on to the cliff face which defended the citadel on that side. A honeysuckle clung to the roof, its flowers reaching down towards the sunlight. A little stream of water trickled over the floor of the cave.

Inside the cave there were perhaps a hundred white horses eating barley from a long plank on a level with their mouths. Their manes were all dyed blue, their hoofs were clad in esparto slippers and the hair between their ears had been curled up over their foreheads like a wig. They had long flowing tails which they flicked lazily over their haunches. The Proconsul gazed at them, speechless with admiration.

They were magnificent creatures, lithe as snakes and light as birds. They could fly as swiftly as their riders' arrows, seize their adversaries wholesale between their teeth and topple them to the floor, run sure-foot over the most difficult rocky terrain, leap over precipices and gallop at full tilt across the plains all day long without tiring. A single word of command would bring them to a halt. As soon as Jacim walked in they came over to him, like sheep at the approach of the shepherd, stretching their necks forward and looking at him with anxious, childlike eyes. Jacim, as he always did, gave a husky, deep-throated cry which clearly delighted them; they reared up on their hind legs, eager to be let loose and to run free.

Antipas had feared that Vitellius would take these horses from him, and had shut them away in the place intended for animals in the event of a siege.

'This is a bad place to stable horses,' said the Proconsul. 'You risk losing them. Sisenna, make an inventory!'

The publican took a tablet from his belt, counted the horses and wrote down the number.

Inspectors from the tax companies invariably tried to bribe governors in order to extort as much as they could from the provinces. This man nosed into everything, his eyes blinking and his mouth twitching like a ferret's.

Eventually they all went back up to the courtyard.

Here and there, set into the paving stones, were little round lids made of bronze that covered the water cisterns. The publican noticed one which was bigger than the others and which gave out a different sound when he walked on it. He went to each of them, striking it in turn and then, prancing up and down, he shouted out:

'I've found it! I've found it! It's Herod's treasure!'

The search for Herod's treasure had become an obsession with the Romans.

The Tetrarch swore that no such treasure had ever existed.

Then what was underneath?

'Nothing! A man, a prisoner.'

'Let us see him!' Vitellius ordered.

The Tetrarch hesitated, knowing that his secret would be revealed to the Jews. Vitellius was becoming irritated by his reluctance to open the lid.

'Break it in!' he called out to the lictors.

Mannaeï had gathered what they had in mind. He saw that they had an axe and suspected that Jokanaan was about to be beheaded. The lictor had landed the first blow on the covering, but Mannaeï stopped him, inserted a kind of hook between it and the paving stones and then, tensing his long thin arms, he gently lifted it until it fell back. Everyone was amazed at the old man's strength. Under the wood-lined cover lay a trapdoor of similar size. Mannaeï struck it sharply with his fist and it fell open in two halves. What they saw now was a hole, a huge pit with a set of unrailed steps winding down into it. Those who were close enough to peer over the edge saw at the bottom a vague shape which terrified them.

A human being lay stretched on the ground, his long hair running down into the hair of the animal hides which covered his back. He got to his feet. His forehead touched the grating which had been fastened horizontally over the pit and from time to time he disappeared back into the depths of his lair.

The sun glinted on the tips of the tiaras and the hilts of the swords; the heat thrown up from the paving stones was intense. Doves flew out from the wall friezes and wheeled above the courtyard. It was at this time of day that Mannaeï usually came to throw down seed for them. He remained crouching in front of the Tetrarch, who was standing close to Vitellius. The Galileans, priests and soldiers stood in a circle behind them. Nobody spoke. Everyone waited anxiously to see what would happen next.

First there came a great, cavernous sigh.

Herodias heard it from the far end of the palace and found herself strangely powerless to resist its summons. She threaded her way through the crowd, placed her hand on Mannaeï's shoulder and leaned forward to listen.

The voice grew louder:

'Woe unto you, all Pharisees and Sadducees, you generation of vipers, you bloated wineskins, you tinkling cymbals!'

Everyone knew that this was Jokanaan. His name was passed from mouth to mouth. Other people came running to listen.

'Woe unto you, O people! Woe unto the traitors of Judah and the drunkards of Ephraim, unto all who live off the fat of the land and are giddy with the fumes of wine!

'May they pass away like the waters that run to the sea, like the snail that melts as it moves, like the stillborn child that sees not the light of day.

'The time is at hand, Moab, when you must hide in the cypress trees like the sparrow and seek refuge in caves like the jerboa. The gates of your citadels shall be rent asunder more swiftly than the cracking of a nut, their walls shall crumble and your cities shall be consumed by fire. The scourge of the Almighty shall not cease! Your limbs shall be turned in your own blood, like wool in a dyer's vat. He shall tear you to pieces as with a new harrow and scatter your flesh in shreds upon the mountains.'

Who was this conqueror that he spoke of? Could it be Vitellius? None but the Romans were capable of such a massacre. People began to protest: 'Enough, enough! Silence him!'

But the voice grew louder:

'The newborn child shall crawl in ashes beside its mother's corpse. Men shall go at night, risking death by the sword to gather food among the ruins. Jackals shall fight over bones in public squares where old men once sat talking in the cool of evening. Your daughters shall drink their own tears and play lute music at the banquets of their new master and the finest of your sons shall have their backs bent double and worn to the bone by burdens too heavy to bear!'

The people recalled the history of their exile and all the trials they had endured. These were the words of the old prophets. The voice of Jokanaan rang in their ears like mighty blows that fell upon them one after another.

But the voice now became gentler, more mellifluous and song-like. It spoke of a deliverance that was at hand, of wonders seen in the skies, of a newborn child that places its arm in the dragon's lair, of gold in the place of clay and the desert blossoming like a rose.

'That which is now worth sixty kikkars shall not be worth one obol. Fountains of milk shall spring from the bare rock; men shall eat their fill and fall asleep in the winepresses! Saviour whom I long to see, when will you come? Even now the peoples of the world bow the knee before you. O son of David, your reign shall know no end!'

The Tetrarch started back. He saw the existence of a son of David as both an insult and a threat.

Jokanaan began to berate Antipas for assuming the title of king:

'There is no other king but the Almighty!' He spoke with scorn of his gardens, his statues and his ivory furniture, comparing him to the ungodly Ahab.[16]

Antipas snapped the cord of the seal which hung from his neck and threw it into the pit, ordering Jokanaan to be silent.

But the voice answered back:

'I will roar like a bear. I will bray like a wild ass and shriek like a woman in labour! Your incest has brought its own retribution. God has afflicted you with the sterility of a mule!'

There was a ripple of laughter, like waves lapping on the shore.

Vitellius was determined to stay and listen. The interpreter calmly repeated in the language of the Romans all the insults that Jokanaan was pouring out in his own, so that the Tetrarch and Herodias had to endure them twice over. He stood there gasping for breath, while she gazed open-mouthed at the bottom of the pit.

This man was fearsome to behold. Throwing his head back, he grasped the bars of the grating and pressed his face against it. They saw what looked like a tangle of brushwood with two burning coals glowing in its midst.

'Ah! It is you, Jezebel! You who stole his heart by the squeak in your shoe! You whinnied like a mare. You set up your bed on the mountain-tops to perform your oblations! But the Lord shall tear away your earrings, your purple robes and your linen veils, the bracelets on your arms, the rings about your feet and the little golden crescents that quiver on your brow, your silver mirrors, your fans of ostrich plumes and the mother-of-pearl pattens which make you seem so tall, your proud display of diamonds, the scents in your hair, the paint on your nails and all the false adornments of your womanhood. There are not enough rocks in all the world for the stoning of adultery like yours!'

She looked around for someone to defend her. The Pharisees lowered their eyes hypocritically. The Sadducees looked away, afraid that they might offend the Proconsul. Antipas looked as though he was about to die.

The voice grew louder still, filling the air and rumbling around them like claps of thunder. Its echo bounced back off the mountains, multiplying itself and shaking Machaerus with redoubled force.

'Prostrate yourself in the dust, O daughter of Babylon! Grind your own meal! Loosen your girdle, take off your shoes, hitch up your skirts and wade through the stream! Your shame shall be seen and your disgrace made known to all! You shall weep with anguish and your teeth shall break in your mouth! The Lord abhors the stench of your crimes! Cursed and twice cursed! May you die like a bitch!'

The trapdoor was shut and the cover fell back into place. Mannaeï wished he could have strangled Jokanaan.

Herodias disappeared. The Pharisees were outraged. Antipas stood in their midst, attempting to explain.

'Certainly a man may marry his brother's wife,' said Eleazar, 'but Herodias was not a widow and what is more she had a child. That is what makes it a sin.'

'No, there you are mistaken,' countered the Sadducee Jonathas. 'The Law disapproves of such marriages but it does not absolutely forbid them.'

'What the Law says is neither here nor there,' said Antipas. 'I am being treated most unfairly! After all, Absalom slept with his father's wives, Judah slept with his daughter-in-law, Ammon slept with his sister and Lot slept with his own daughters.'

Just at this moment, Aulus, who had been asleep, reappeared. When they had explained what the argument was all about he sided with the Tetrarch. He said that they should not get so upset about such trifles and he laughed out loud at the priests' disapproval and Jokanaan's anger.

Herodias was half-way up the steps. She turned towards him. 'You have no cause to laugh, my lord,' she said to Aulus. 'Jokanaan is telling the people not to pay their taxes.'

The publican asked them straight away if this was true.

Most of them said that it was true and the Tetrarch himself agreed.

It occurred to Vitellius that the prisoner might escape and that Antipas was behaving strangely. So he posted sentries at the gates, all along the walls and round the courtyard.

Then he went off towards his rooms, accompanied by the deputations of priests.

They all had grievances to air, although no one raised the issue of the High Priesthood. Every one of them insisted on being heard. Eventually Vitellius sent them all away.

Jonathas was just leaving him when he noticed Antipas standing in a corner of the castle wall and talking with a long-haired man dressed in white – an Essene. He began to wish he had not taken his side.

There was one thing that Antipas could take comfort from. Jokanaan was no longer his responsibility; the Romans would deal with him. And that was a great relief! Phanuel happened to be walking along the battlements. Antipas called him over and pointed at the soldiers.

'They are stronger than I am,' he said. 'I cannot set him free. There is nothing I can do about it!'

The courtyard was now empty. The slaves were taking their rest. A fiery red glow lit up the sky on the horizon. Anything that stood upright was silhouetted against it in black. Antipas could make out the saltworks at the far end of the Dead Sea but he could no longer see the Arabs' tents. They must have gone, he thought. The moon was rising and a feeling of great calm came over him.

Phanuel stood beside him, utterly overcome, his chin sunk upon his breast. At last he told Antipas what was on his mind.

Since the beginning of the month he had been getting up before dawn to study the heavens, as the constellation of Perseus was at its zenith. Agala was scarcely visible, Algol was less bright than usual and Mira Ceti had disappeared altogether. From this he prophesied the death of an important person that very night in Machaerus.

Who might it be? Vitellius was too well guarded and they were certainly not going to execute Jokanaan. 'Then it must be me,' thought the Tetrarch.

Perhaps the Arabs were going to come back. Maybe the Proconsul would find out about his dealings with the Parthians! The priests were escorted by hired assassins from Jerusalem who had daggers hidden in their clothing. As for Phanuel's ability to read the stars, the Tetrarch had no doubts about it whatsoever.

Perhaps Herodias could help him. He hated her, it was true, but he knew that she could give him some moral support and the spell of his old attachment to her was not entirely broken.

As he entered her room, cinnamon smoke rose from a porphyry bowl. Powders, unguents, drapes that floated like clouds and embroideries light as birds' feathers lay everywhere.

He did not mention Phanuel's prediction or his own fears about the Jews and the Arabs. She would have accused him of being a coward. He spoke only of the Romans. Vitellius had told him nothing about his military plans. Antipas suspected he was in league with Caius, who was a close friend of Agrippa, and that they were planning to send him into exile. He might even end up having his throat slit.

Herodias, with an affected sympathy that barely disguised her contempt, tried to allay his fears. Eventually she took a strange-looking medal from a little box. Engraved on it was a portrait of Tiberius. This, she said, was all he needed to make the lictors turn pale and to silence their accusations.

Antipas, overcome with gratitude, asked her how she had come by it.

'It was given to me,' she said.

From under a curtain facing them a bare arm emerged, a young and very attractive arm which might have been carved in ivory by Polyclitus.[17] It groped around, rather awkwardly yet at the same time with perfect grace, feeling for a tunic that had been left on a stool by the wall.

An old woman drew the curtain aside and passed the tunic through.

The Tetrarch remembered something he had seen not long before, but he could not quite place it.

'Is that slave yours?' he asked.

'What does it matter to you?' Herodias replied.

3

The banqueting hall was now filled with guests.

It had three aisles like a basilica, separated by sandalwood pillars with capitals richly carved in bronze. The pillars supported two clerestory galleries. A third gallery, ornamented with gold filigree, formed a semicircle at one end of the hall directly facing a huge rounded apse at the other end.

Glowing candelabra stood on the tables, which had been set out in rows from one end of the hall to the other, and formed branched clusters of light amidst the cups of painted earthenware, the copper dishes, the blocks of snow and the huge piles of grapes. Because of the great height of the ceiling, the red glow from the candles gradually faded as it rose and was broken into little points of light that shone like stars in the night through the branches of trees. Through the great bay window lighted torches could be seen on the terraces of the houses, for Antipas was also offering this feast to his friends, his subjects and everyone else who had come to Machaerus.

Slaves, watchful as dogs and their feet clad in felt sandals, moved from table to table bearing platters of food.

The Proconsul's table stood beneath the golden gallery on a raised platform made of sycamore. Babylonian carpets had been hung around it to form a sort of tent.

There were three ivory couches for Vitellius, his son and Antipas, one facing the hall and one at each side; the Proconsul sat on the left near to the door, Aulus sat on the right and the Tetrarch in the middle.

He was wearing a heavy black cloak, with the colour so richly applied that it was impossible to say what material it was made of. He had put rouge on his cheeks, combed his beard in the shape of a fan, powdered his hair blue and fastened it with a jewelled diadem. Vitellius still wore his purple laticlave draped diagonally across his linen toga. Aulus wore a robe of violet silk threaded with silver, with its sleeves tied behind his back. The ringlets of his hair were arranged in layers and a sapphire necklace sparkled on his breast, which was as white and well rounded as a woman's. Close beside him, sitting cross-legged on a mat, was a very beautiful young boy, with a permanent smile on his face. Aulus had noticed him in the kitchens and could not bear to be parted from him. He found it difficult to remember his Chaldean name[18] and referred to him simply as 'Asiaticus'. From time to time Aulus lay back at full length on his couch so that all that could be seen of him was his bare feet.

On his side of the hall were the priests and the Tetrarch's officers, some citizens of Jerusalem and the leaders of the Greek cities. On the Proconsul's side were Marcellus and the publicans, some of the Tetrarch's friends and dignitaries from Cana, Ptolemais and Jericho. Then, seated at random, there were mountaineers from the Lebanon, Herod's old soldiers – twelve Thracians, one Gaul and two Germans – some gazelle hunters, some shepherds from Idumaea, the Sultan of Palmyra and some sailors from Ezion-gaber. Everyone was provided with a cake of soft pastry to wipe their fingers on; arms stretched across the tables like vultures' necks to take helpings of olives, pistachio-nuts and almonds. Every face glowed with pleasure from beneath its garland of flowers.

The Pharisees had refused to wear these, considering them to be Roman obscenities, and they shuddered when they were sprinkled with galbanum and incense, a mixture which they reserved for the rites of the Temple.

Aulus rubbed it into his armpits; Antipas promised to send him a whole supply of it, along with three basketfuls of the original balsam that had made Cleopatra so long to be the queen of Palestine.

A captain from his garrison at Tiberias, who had arrived only a few moments earlier, came to stand behind Antipas to tell him of certain extraordinary events that had occurred there, but the Tetrarch was too absorbed in attending to the Proconsul and listening to what was being said at the tables in front of him.

They were talking about Jokanaan and others like him; Simon of Gitta who cleansed sins by fire and a certain Jesus . . .

'He is the worst of all,' exclaimed Eleazar. 'A cheap charlatan!'

Behind the Tetrarch, a man rose to his feet, his face as white as the hem of his mantle. He stepped down from the platform and addressed the Pharisees:

'That is a lie,' he said. 'Jesus performs miracles!'

Antipas said that he would like to see them for himself.

'You should have brought him with you! Tell us about him!'

The man then explained how he, Jacob, had gone to Capernaum when his daughter had fallen ill and had begged the Master to heal her. 'Go back to your house,' the Master had told him. 'Your daughter is cured!' And he had found her waiting for him at their door, having risen from her sickbed at the third hour, as indicated by the palace sundial, the very moment at which he had spoken to Jesus.

But the Pharisees were not convinced. Certainly there were practical remedies and there were potent medicinal herbs. Here at Machaerus itself you could sometimes find the baaras plant, whose leaves were a protection against all ills. But to heal someone without even seeing or touching them was impossible, unless of course Jesus employed demons.

The Tetrarch's friends, the chief men of Galilee, all nodded their heads in agreement.

'Yes,' they said, 'he must be using demons.'

Jacob, who was standing between their table and that of the priests, said nothing, looking at them with a mixture of pity and scorn.

They insisted that he tell them more. 'How do you explain his power?'

He bent his shoulders and speaking quietly and deliberately, as though afraid of himself, he said:

'Do you not realize that he is the Messiah?'

The priests looked askance at each other; Vitellius asked what this word meant. His interpreter hesitated before replying.

It was a word used to describe a liberator, someone who would restore to them all that was rightfully theirs and give them dominion over all other peoples. Some even argued that there would be two Messiahs. The first of them would be overthrown by Gog and Magog, demons of the North, but the second would slay the Prince of Evil. His coming had been awaited day by day for centuries.

The priests quickly conferred amongst themselves. Eleazar then spoke on their behalf.

In the first place, the Messiah was to be a son of David, not the son of a carpenter. Secondly, the Messiah would uphold the Law, whereas this Nazarene attacked it. Finally, and this was the strongest of their arguments, the Messiah would be preceded by the coming of Elijah.[19]

'But Elijah is already with us,' replied Jacob.

'Elijah! Elijah!' chanted the crowd from one end of the hall to the other.

In their mind's eye, everyone pictured an old man with ravens circling above him, an altar set on fire by lightning, idolatrous priests flung into raging streams. The women seated in the galleries thought of the widow of Sarepta.[20]

Try as he might, Jacob could not convince them that he knew who Elijah was, that he had seen him and that the people had seen him too.

'Then name him,' they cried.

'His name is Jokanaan!' shouted Jacob at the top of his voice.

Antipas fell back as if he had been struck full in the chest. The Sadducees rushed at Jacob. Eleazar continued to declaim out loud, trying to make himself heard above the noise.

When silence had returned, he wrapped his cloak around him and began to ask questions like a judge.

'Seeing that the prophet is dead . . .'

He was interrupted by murmurs of disapproval. People believed that Elijah had merely disappeared.

Eleazar turned angrily upon the crowd and continued with his questions:

'Do you think that he has risen from the dead?'

'Why not?' answered Jacob.

The Sadducees shrugged their shoulders. Jonathas, his tiny eyes wide open, gave a forced laugh like a circus clown. Nothing could be more foolish than to claim that the body possessed eternal life and, for the benefit of the Proconsul, he recited the following verse by a contemporary poet:

Nec crescit, nec post mortem durare videtur.[21]

But Aulus was leaning over the edge of his couch, his forehead bathed in sweat, his face green and his hands clutching his stomach.

The Sadducees put on a show of great concern for him (the very next day the High Priesthood was restored to them). Antipas pretended to be distraught. Vitellius seemed unmoved. His concern was very real, however, for if he lost his son he would lose his fortune.

Aulus had scarcely finished making himself sick before he wanted to start eating again.

'Bring me grated marble,' he cried. 'Bring me schist from Naxos or water from the sea! Bring me whatever you want! Or perhaps I should take a bath?'

He bit into a large lump of snow and then, being unable to decide whether to eat a Commagene terrine or some ouzels, he opted for pumpkins in honey. Asiaticus gazed at him in wonder, convinced that this propensity for self-indulgence marked him out as a superior being of the highest pedigree.

While the guests were being served with ox-kidneys, dormice, nightingales and minced meat wrapped in vine leaves, the priests debated the problem of resurrection. Ammonius, a pupil of Philo the Platonist, thought they were stupid and said so to some Greeks who were joking about oracles. Marcellus had come over to join Jacob and was telling him of the joys he had experienced as a baptized follower of Mithras. Jacob urged him to follow Jesus. Palm and tamarisk wines, the wines of Safed and Byblos, flowed from jars into bowls, from bowls into cups and from cups into thirsty mouths. Soon everyone was chatting away happily with their neighbours and beginning to relax. Jacim, although he was a Jew, was saying how he still worshipped the planets. A merchant from Aphek was regaling a group of nomads with a detailed account of the marvels of the temple at Hierapolis and they were asking him how much a pilgrimage there would cost. Others were perfectly happy with the religion of their own country. A German who was nearly blind sang a hymn in praise of the promontory in Scandinavia

where the gods appear in shining glory, and there were some
people from Sichem who would not eat turtle doves, as a mark
of respect for the dove Azima.

Several of the guests stood talking to each other in the middle
of the hall, their breath mingling with the smoke from the
candelabra and hanging in the air like fog. Phanuel entered and
walked around the edge of the room. He had just been studying
the heavens again but did not want to walk over to the Tetrarch
in case he was splashed with oil, which the Essenes regarded as
a defilement.

Suddenly a loud knocking was heard on the castle gate.

Word had spread that Jokanaan was being held prisoner there
and men with lighted torches were making their way up the
path. At the foot of the hill could be seen the dark shapes of
many others. From time to time a cry rang out:

'Jokanaan! Jokanaan!'

'He is nothing but trouble!' said Jonathas.

'If things go on like this,' added the Pharisees, 'we shall all be
left destitute!'

The accusations came thick and fast.

'We need protection!'

'Do away with him!'

'You have no respect for religion!'

'You are as ungodly as all the other Herods!'

'But not as ungodly as you!' retorted Antipas. 'It was my
father who rebuilt your temple!'

Then the Pharisees, the sons of the outlawed followers of the
two Matathiases, began to accuse the Tetrarch of all his family's
crimes.

They had sharp pointed heads, great bristling beards and
flabby, evil-looking hands. There were others among them who
looked like bulldogs, with short snub noses and big round eyes.
A dozen or so of them, some scribes and some of the priests'
servants, who lived off the leftovers from burnt sacrifices, rushed
up to the foot of the platform and threatened Antipas with
their knives. Antipas rebuked them while the Sadducees made a
half-hearted attempt to defend him. He caught sight of Mannaeï
and with a wave of his hand told him to go away since it was

quite clear from the expression on the face of Vitellius that he felt this was none of his business.

The Pharisees who had remained on their couches suddenly began to rant and rave as if they were possessed by demons, smashing their plates on the table in front of them. They had been served with wild-ass stew, a favourite dish of Maecenas but one which they considered to be unclean.

Aulus jokingly reminded them of the ass's head that everyone said they worshipped and made other sarcastic comments about their aversion to pigs. No doubt it was only because some overfed pig had killed their 'Bacchus' – and since the discovery of a golden vine in the Temple, their fondness for wine was an open secret.

The priests did not understand what he was saying. Phineas, a Galilean by birth, refused to translate, which angered Aulus intensely, all the more so as Asiaticus had run away in terror. The meal was not to his liking, the food was the sort that common people ate and it needed more flavouring! He calmed down a little at the sight of some Syrian sheeps' tails, the greasiest dish that could be imagined.

Vitellius found the Jews repulsive. He suspected that they worshipped Moloch[22] as he had come across several altars to this god on his way to Machaerus. He called to mind stories of child sacrifice and a man who had been mysteriously fattened up. Being a Roman, he found their intolerance, their mad iconoclastic frenzy and their mulish obstinacy sickening. He decided it was time to leave. Aulus, however, wanted to stay.

He was lying flat on his back behind a huge pile of food with his robe hanging around his waist, too bloated to eat any more yet unable to tear himself away from the table.

The people grew more and more excited. They began to talk about their hopes of independence, recalling Israel's glorious past. Every conqueror of Israel had been duly punished – Antigonus, Crassus, Varus . . .

'Shame on you!' said the Proconsul, for he understood Syriac; his only reason for having an interpreter was that it gave him more time to prepare his answers.

Antipas hurriedly took out the medal of the Emperor, his

hand shaking as he looked at it. He showed it to Vitellius, with the face of the Emperor uppermost.

Suddenly the panels in the golden balcony were folded back and Herodias appeared in a blaze of candlelight, surrounded by slaves and festoons of anemones. On her head she wore an Assyrian mitre held in place by a chin strap. Her hair fell in long ringlets on to a scarlet peplum which was split down the length of each sleeve. Standing as she was between two monstrous creatures carved in stone that stood on either side of the doorway like those guarding the treasure of Atreus, she looked like Cybele with her attendant lions. She stood on the balcony directly above Antipas, holding a patera between both hands, and declaimed:

'Long live Caesar!'

The cry was taken up by Vitellius, Antipas and the priests.

At the same time, from the far end of the hall, came a buzz of surprise and admiration. A young girl had just come in.

A blue-tinted veil covered her head and breasts. Through it could be glimpsed the curve of her eyes, the chalcedony jewels that hung from her ears and the whiteness of her body. A drape of dove-coloured silk fell from her shoulders and was fastened about her thighs with a jewelled girdle. She wore dark-coloured trousers embellished with mandrakes. She moved forward with languid grace, tapping the floor with her tiny slippers of hummingbirds' down.

She went up on to the platform and slipped off her veil. It might have been Herodias, as she used to be in her youth. Then she began to dance.

Her feet moved rhythmically one in front of the other to the sounds of a flute and a pair of hand cymbals. She extended her arms in a circle, as if she were calling to someone who was fleeing her approach. She ran after him, light as a butterfly, like Psyche[23] in search of her lover, a soul adrift, as if she were about to take flight.

The sound of the cymbals gave way to the more sombre notes of the flute. Hope had ceded to grief. Her movements now suggested sighs and her whole body took on an attitude of such languor that one could not tell whether she was mourning a departed god or expiring in his embrace. With her eyes half-closed, she swivelled her waist, thrust her belly backwards and forwards in rhythmic waves and made her breasts quiver; her face remained expressionless but her feet never stopped moving.

Vitellius compared her to Mnester, the mime actor. Aulus was being sick again. The Tetrarch was lost in a dream and had stopped thinking about Herodias. He imagined he saw her standing near the Sadducees, but the vision quickly faded from his mind.

Yet what he had seen was no mere figment of the imagination. Herodias had had her daughter Salome brought up far from Machaerus, knowing that one day the Tetrarch would fall in love with her. It was a clever move and she now knew that her plan was working.

The dance continued, now depicting the lover's yearning for satisfaction. She danced like the priestesses of the Indies, like the Nubian girls of the cataracts, like the bacchantes of Lydia. Her body twisted in every direction like a flower buffeted by the storm. The jewels that hung from her ears danced about her face, her silken shift shimmered in the light, and from her arms, her feet and her clothing leapt unseen sparks that enflamed the hearts of the men who watched her. A harp played sweet music and the crowd responded with shouts of acclamation. Without bending her knees, she spread her legs apart and inclined her body so low that her chin touched the floor. Nomads weaned on abstinence, Roman soldiers practised in debauchery, mean-minded publicans and priests embittered by religious wrangling, all looked on, their nostrils dilated, quivering with desire.

Next she danced in a circle around the Tetrarch's table, spinning wildly on her feet like the humming-top of a sorceress. 'Come to my arms!' cried Antipas, in a voice choking with passion. She continued to dance before him, while the drums beat furiously and the crowd roared. The Tetrarch's voice rose above the din. 'Come to my arms! You shall have Capernaum! The plain of Tiberias! All my citadels! Half my kingdom!'

She threw herself on her hands with her heels in the air and in this pose she crossed from one side of the platform to the other like an enormous beetle. Then suddenly she stood absolutely still.

Her neck and her spine formed a perfect right angle. The coloured silks which she wore about her legs fell down over her shoulders like rainbows and encircled her face just a few inches from the ground. Her lips were painted red, her eyebrows black; she had startling dark eyes; tiny beads of sweat clung to her brow like droplets of water on white marble.

She said nothing. She and the Tetrarch stood looking into each other's eyes.

There was a snapping of fingers from the balcony above. She went up to the balcony and then came back to stand in front of Antipas. With a look of childish innocence and a slight lisp in her voice she spoke the following words:

'I want you to give me on a plate the head of . . .' She had forgotten the name. Then, with a smile, she continued: 'The head of Jokanaan!'

The Tetrarch sank back on his couch, stunned.

He was bound by his word and the people awaited his reply. It occurred to him that if the death which Phanuel had predicted happened to someone else, at least his own death might be averted. If Jokanaan really was Elias, he would find a way of avoiding it. If he was not, then the murder was of no consequence.

Mannaeï, standing beside him, understood what he was required to do.

Vitellius called him back to tell him the password for the sentries guarding the pit.

Antipas felt relieved. In a moment it would all be over.

But for Mannaeï the task was not as easy as expected.

He reappeared, obviously disturbed.

For forty years he had performed the duties of executioner. It was he who had drowned Aristobulus, strangled Alexander, burnt Matathias alive and beheaded Soaemus, Pappus, Joseph and Antipater. And now he could not bring himself to kill Jokanaan! His teeth were chattering and his whole body shook.

In front of the pit he had seen the Great Angel of the Samaritans, covered with eyes and brandishing a huge sword, red and jagged like a tongue of flame. He had brought two soldiers back with him as witnesses and they would bear him out.

But they said they had seen nothing except a Jewish captain who had rushed at them and who was now no more.

Herodias vented her anger in a stream of coarse and unseemly abuse. She broke her fingernails as she clutched the railing of the balcony; the two carved lions seemed to be snapping at her shoulders and roaring with her.

Antipas did likewise, along with the priests, the soldiers and the Pharisees, all calling for vengeance, while the rest objected noisily at having their pleasure delayed.

Mannaeï went out, hiding his face.

This time the guests found the wait even longer than before and they began to get impatient.

Suddenly they heard the clatter of footsteps in the corridors outside. The tension became unbearable.

Then, in came the head – Mannaeï holding it aloft by the hair and proudly acknowledging the applause which greeted him.

He put it on a plate and gave it to Salome, who carried it nimbly up the steps to the balcony.

A few minutes later, the head was brought back, carried by the old woman that the Tetrarch had noticed sitting on the roof of a house that morning and again later, in Herodias' room.

Antipas stepped back so as not to see it. Vitellius gave it a cursory glance.

Mannaeï stepped down from the platform and displayed the head to the Roman captains, and then to everyone who was dining on that side of the hall.

They all had a close look at it.

The sharp blade of the sword, as it was brought down on to the head, had sliced into the jaw. The corners of the mouth were drawn back in a grimace. The beard was spattered with clots of already congealed blood. The closed eyelids were as pale as shells. The head was bathed in the light of the candelabra that shone around it.

It was brought to the table where the priests were sitting. One of the Pharisees turned it over to have a closer look at it. Mannaeï set it upright again and placed it in front of Aulus, who woke up with a start. From between their lashes, the eyes of the dead man and the eyes of the sluggard seemed to be saying something to each other.

Finally Mannaeï presented the head to Antipas. Tears were streaming down the Tetrarch's face.

The torches were extinguished. The guests left, leaving only Antipas in the hall. He stood with his head in his hands, still gazing at the severed head. In the centre of the great nave, Phanuel, with his arms extended, muttered prayers to himself.

Just as the sun was rising, two men, who had been sent off in search of information by Jokanaan some time before, returned with the long-awaited news.

They confided it to Phanuel, who was overjoyed.

Then he showed them the gruesome object on the plate among the remains of the banquet. One of the men said:

'Have no fear! He has gone down among the dead to proclaim the coming of Christ!'

And then the Essene understood the meaning of the words: 'If his reign is to come, mine must end.'

They picked up Jokanaan's head and all three went off in the direction of Galilee.

Because the head was very heavy, they took it in turns to carry it.

Notes

A SIMPLE HEART

1. *just one hundred francs a year*: Félicité's very modest earnings are the equivalent of around £1,000 a year. Her mistress's annual income from farm rents is the equivalent of £50,000 a year.
2. *Pont-l'Evêque ... Toucques and Geffosses*: The tale is set in the landscape of Flaubert's childhood, a small area just inland from the seaside village of Trouville, on the Normandy coast. Place-names and topographical details are all authentic. Precise imaginative reminiscence lends this tale its special richness of feeling.
3. *The clock ... designed to look like a Temple of Vesta*: The Temple of Vesta stood near the river Tiber in Rome. It was a relatively modest circular building with a shallow conical roof and twenty slender fluted columns with Corinthian capitals. The temple housed the sacred hearth where the Vestal Virgins kept an eternal fire burning. In this context, the clock is a fine example of bourgeois neo-classical style.
4. *etchings by Audran*: Jean Audran (1667–1756) produced engraved copies of paintings by Italian and French masters. In this context, his etchings signify good taste.
5. *thirty sous*: The equivalent of about £5.
6. *his parents had paid for someone else to do his military service*: Military service was decided by annual lottery. It was customary, in the early decades of the nineteenth century, for young men who drew a high number in the lottery to pay for a substitute to do their military service.
7. *he would go to the Préfecture*: The Préfecture was the centre of local administration. Conscription was organized at the Préfecture.
8. *Paul and Virginie*: These two names had an archetypal resonance for the nineteenth-century reader. They are taken from Bernardin

de Saint-Pierre's bestselling brother-and-sister tale, *Paul et Virginie* (1787).

9. *to play Boston*: Boston whist was the eighteenth-century ancestor of bridge.

10. *Trouville*: A fishing-village on the Normandy coast, Trouville was 'discovered' in the 1830s and became fashionable with Parisians for its spacious sandy beaches and its cliff walks. When Flaubert was a boy, his family usually spent their summer holidays in Trouville.

11. *she had to take Virginie to catechism*: Classes of elementary religious education, in preparation for a child's first communion, an important rite of passage.

12. *made an altar of repose*: During the feast of Corpus Christi, a popular summer festival, the sacrament was paraded through the streets, pausing at a series of temporary altars, all of them elaborately decorated.

13. *the Ursuline convent school in Honfleur*: Honfleur is 10 miles from Pont l'Evêque, a journey of several hours in the early decades of the nineteenth century. The education of middle-class girls, still in the hands of the Church, was conducted in fiercely conservative convent schools.

14. *the Calvary*: A large wayside crucifix, like a signpost; in this context the symbol of popular religious devotion.

15. *lye*: An alkaline solution made with water and vegetable ashes, then used as a detergent.

16. *She had a standing arrangement with a job-master*: A job-master kept a livery stable, hiring out horses and carriages.

17. *the July Revolution*: King Charles X, an ultra-royalist, was deposed to great liberal rejoicing in July 1830.

18. *terrible atrocities in '93*: The year 1793 – forty years ago, in the story – was the year of the Terror, notorious in popular memory for its ruthless political murders.

19. *her husband had been promoted to a Préfecture*: A Prefect administered a whole region, in the name of central government.

20. *and eventually reached Saint-Gatien*: Félicité's encounter with the mail-coach is a hidden reference to Flaubert's first epileptic attack, which occurred on the same spot in January 1844.

21. *the Comte d'Artois*: King Charles X, formerly Comte d'Artois, came to the throne in 1824 and was deposed in 1830.

22. *Epinal colour print*: Brightly coloured popular prints, often on religious or nationalist themes, they were named after the town of Epinal in north-eastern France.

23. *discovered his vocation – the Registry Office!*: A very minor civil service post. Paul is being mocked for the modesty of his ambitions.

24. *bandeaux*: A respectable style, with the hair worn in coils.

25. *a pension of three hundred and eighty francs*: Less than four years' wages for fifty years of service, implicitly a very meagre bequest.

26. *the Holy Sacrament, which was carried by Monsieur le Curé*: A respectful reference to the village priest, in surreptitious mimicry of Félicité's pious idiom.

27. *ophicleides*: A deep wind instrument, like a bass version of the bugle.

THE LEGEND OF SAINT JULIAN HOSPITATOR

A 'hospitator' is one who provides lodging. The French title refers to Saint Julian as 'l'Hospitalier', a term which would normally refer to a religious order such as the Knights Hospitallers. There is no clear evidence in the story or in Flaubert's sources that Julian ever becomes a member of a religious order. Thus the title 'Hospitator' is unique to him and his chosen mode of penance.

1. *mall*: Sometimes referred to as 'pall-mall', a game in which players, using a mallet, attempt to strike a wooden ball through a suspended iron ring.

2. *his vassals*: His feudal inferiors, tenants who owed him their allegiance.

3. *scallop-shells*: The scallop-shell was worn as the badge of a Christian pilgrim who had been to the shrine of St James of Compostela.

4. *he would dip into his purse*: By thus giving money to the poor, Julian is practising the virtue of charity.

5. *almost exactly as you will find it told in a stained-glass window in a church near to where I was born*: There is a Saint Julian window in Rouen cathedral, half a mile from where Flaubert was born. The window tells the story of the saint in an elaborate series of small panels. Flaubert liked to emphasize the discrepancies between the window and his story. He authorized a contemporary edition of this tale with a black-and-white line-drawing of the window. Looking at the image, the reader would be puzzled, asking 'How on earth did *this* come from *that*?'

Above the main door of the same cathedral there is also a bas-relief depicting Salome dancing before Herod.

HERODIAS

'Herodias' is set in Judaea (southern Palestine) at the time of Jesus' ministry. Subject to Rome, the Jewish people are smouldering with messianic hopes of liberation. Herod-Antipas, their puppet-king, the protagonist of this tale, is scheming to ensure his own political survival. Antipas has divorced his first wife, daughter of the king of the adjacent desert kingdom, in order to marry his niece Herodias, formerly the wife of his half-brother. The marriage has offended his former father-in-law and alienated his Jewish subjects. Jokanaan (John the Baptist), a radical Jewish religious leader, has publicly reproached Antipas for this marriage, insisting that it transgresses Mosaic law. Herodias has pushed her husband into imprisoning Jokanaan. This is the point at which the story begins.

1. *citadel of Machaerus*: The citadel of Machaerus (present-day Mekaur) is of great political significance. It controls the cross-roads between the continents of Asia, Africa and Europe. A symbol of secular power, the citadel is set against the distant vision of the temple in Jerusalem, some 20 miles away across the Dead Sea. Flaubert had seen this exotic landscape at first hand.

2. *Perhaps Agrippa had spoken ill of him to the Emperor*: Herod Agrippa was a cousin of Antipas. Agrippa lived in Rome and schemed against Antipas.

3. *during the reign of King Hyrcanus*: Hyrcanus was high priest and ruler of the Jewish nation from 135 to 104 BC.

4. *If his reign is to come, mine must end!*: See the words of John the Baptist in the Bible: 'He must increase, but I must decrease' (John 3: 30).

5. *he wanted Caius to be Emperor*: Caius, the future emperor Caligula, was a close friend of Agrippa. As emperor-in-waiting, Caius attracted many plots, and Agrippa was involved in one of these.

6. *they saw an Essene coming towards them*: Subsequently referred to as Phanuel, the Essene is a member of a Jewish secret society, once thought to be connected with John the Baptist and with Jesus.

7. *prophecies made in the time of Nehemiah*: Nehemiah lived in the fifth century BC, more than four hundred years earlier. The

prophecies said that Elijah would return, bringing the Messiah.

8. *Vitellius*: As the political representative of Roman power, Vitellius holds the office of proconsul, or provincial governor.

9. *laticlave*: A badge consisting of two broad purple stripes on the edge of the tunic, worn by senators and others of high rank.

10. *great King Herod*: Vitellius responds to Antipas' eulogy by praising not Antipas but Antipas' father, King Herod, which amounts to answering a compliment with an insult.

11. *'Even if you go behind someone else's back?'*: Vitellius had concluded a treaty with the king of the Parthians, but Antipas had managed to steal the credit for it.

12. *This flower from the gutters of Capri*: The Emperor Tiberius had a villa on the island of Capri. It was the scene of notorious orgies, in which Aulus played a prominent role.

13. *publicans*: Tax-gatherers.

14. *velites*: Lightly armed soldiers.

15. *Aulus could not contain himself*: Aulus Vitellius, later emperor (AD 69), was famed for his gluttony.

16. *comparing him to the ungodly Ahab*: Ahab was king of Israel in the ninth century BC. Ahab's Phoenician queen, Jezebel, antagonized the people by imposing worship of a foreign god, Baal. Ahab was subsequently denounced by the prophet Elijah. See 1 Kings 16–21.

17. *Polyclitus*: A Greek sculptor of the fifth century BC who specialized in graceful statues of young athletes.

18. *his Chaldean name*: Chaldea, frequently mentioned in the Old Testament, was situated in modern southern Iraq.

19. *Elijah*: The greatest of the prophets of Israel.

20. *In their mind's eye ... the widow of Sarepta*: Three incidents from the life of Elijah, as recounted in the First Book of Kings. The ravens fed Elijah while he was hiding in the desert. Elijah humiliated the priests of the rival god Baal when Elijah's sacrifice was consumed by fire from heaven after that of Baal's priests failed to ignite. The widow of Sarepta was miraculously able to feed Elijah from her meagre store.

21. *Nec crescit ... videtur*: 'After death, the body is seen neither to grow nor to remain' (Lucretius, *De Rerum Natura*, iii. 339).

22. *they worshipped Moloch*: Moloch was a deity to whom child sacrifices were made throughout the ancient Middle East. Mosaic law forbade the Jewish people to worship Moloch.

23. *Psyche*: In classical mythology, Psyche is the beautiful maiden

who wanders the earth in search of her lover Cupid. 'Psyche' in Greek means 'soul'. Psyche began to be depicted as a human woman in the fifth century BC; previously the soul had been represented as a bird or a butterfly.